Nona Nance is a mother of four, grandmother of ten, and great-grandmother of five. She enjoys many activities with family such as boating, water and snow skiing and attending Street Rod Car Shows with her husband.

Since raising her children and retiring from a career in accounting, she began practicing the art of quilt making and writing. Writing began as a therapy, recording memories, then after a creative writing class, wrote and completed a novel.

This writing is dedicated to my family, whose interest in literature and learning encourages me to read and continue learning.

Nona Nance

LITTLE TIME

AUSTIN MACAULEY PUBLISHERS™

LONDON • CAMBRIDGE • NEW YORK • SHARJAH

Ordering Information
Quantity sales: Special discounts are available on quantity purchases by corporations, associations, and others. For details, contact the publisher at the address below.

Publisher's Cataloging-in-Publication data
Nance, Nona
Little Time

ISBN 9781685625849 (Paperback)
ISBN 9781685625856 (ePub e-book)

Library of Congress Control Number: 2023911890

www.austinmacauley.com/us

First Published 2024
Austin Macauley Publishers LLC
40 Wall Street 33rd Floor, Suite 3302
New York, NY 10005
USA

mail-usa@austinmacauley.com
+1 (646) 5125767

I Corinthians 13: 4–8

Love is patient; love is kind; love is not envious or boastful or arrogant or rude. It does not insist on its own way; it is not irritable or resentful; it does not rejoice in wrongdoing, but rejoices in the truth. It bears all things, believes all things, hopes all things, endures all things. Love never ends.

Love is an emotion, a thought, a feeling that is necessary for life to progress, which keeps the world turning. Sometimes we do not recognize love when it slaps us in the face. It may take years for love to grow from a tiny seedling; or this beautiful feeling may pounce on a person the way flowers pop out in the spring and can disappear as quickly as it arrived. Predicting how and when romantic love will develop in a person's life is not to be done. One must be aware of their own emotions in order to engage in any given situation as it comes to them. They must then nurture this feeling so that the love will blossom and grow, embrace each and every situation as though it were the first and last chance. Life is short and often there is little time to dwell on what, when, where, and how love is to be found.

This book is a work of fiction based on living life, growth, family, and love. All names are fictional. The purpose of this narrative is to simulate the growth of a girl's experience in love, and life as it played out for her, as life progressed for her and others close to her, and the most devastating experience of the death of one who touched her heart.

The experience of family love, first love, mutual love, God's love, and love of life is unique to each and everyone. Each of us has a love story or lack of love in their own life. Love affects each person differently, never two be the same.

Part I

Yvonne sleeps peacefully as a vision fills her mind of Jesus knocking on the front door. She can see him at the door and listens as he knocks. As this vision appears, she awakens to the sound of knocking on the front door of her house. The bedroom is on the second floor directly above the front door. The sudden awakening is confusing to her as to whether she actually heard the knocking or if it was just in her dream. Trying to sleep this night was a bit of a struggle as her husband, Joe, had not called her even once during the day or evening, to inform her of any development he had encountered with his work. Nor had he returned home with any explanation of the health report he may have received on his first day back at work.

Confusion muddled her mind as to what she thought she had heard and seen. Again, she heard knocking, and realized someone was actually at the front door of the house. She had no idea what time it might be, but it was dark. She had no idea how long she had been sleeping. Peeping out the window, she tried to get a glimpse of who might be there, but could not see anyone from the upstairs window. The glow from the moon made only a hint of light in the darkness. *Who could possibly be waking her at this time? Was Joe locked out of the house?* She threw on a housecoat as she scurried down the stairs, hoping that the children would not be disturbed from their sleep. She quickly opened the door before anyone could knock again.

As Yvonne peered out into the night, she saw three men standing on the porch. *What could this mean? What is going on? Who are these men?* Her mind became a whirl of questions as one of the men spoke to her. "Mrs. Joe Small?" he began.

"Yes," she replied in almost a whisper.

"Madam, I'm sorry to inform you that there has been an accident." The officer was speaking as he stepped back and forth from one foot to the other.

"Ohh…" came softly out of her mouth as she took a breath. She was trying to concentrate on what the officer was saying, but was having trouble connecting the dots to make sense of this unexpected visit from these three men. She continued to stare at them trying to figure out who they might be.

"Madam," he said again, "I'm sorry to inform you that Joseph Small was in an accident." He said it quickly and quietly as if it wouldn't sound too terrible.

"Ohhh," she breathed out again as she placed her hand in front of her mouth. Her stomach flipped and her body began to shake.

"Yes ma'am, I'm sorry to tell you that, ah, ah, he did not survive." He stuttered, and then relaxed a little as the words finally came out. He had spoken the words which he had not wanted to say.

What did he say? She thought. *Did he say Joe is dead? Can that be true?* She stared at the three of them. One of the men asked, "Are you all right, ma'am?"

All right, how can I be all right if what he says is true? What should I answer? What are they talking about? What happened to Joe? Many, many thoughts began to swirl in her mind as a tornado swiftly gaining speed. She wanted to yell out that they must have the wrong house, or wrong person, or that they should just go away. They stood there looking at her, waiting for what?

"Ma'am, is there someone we could call to come be with you?"

"No" was all she could come out with. Stunned and shocked, she stood there motionless waiting for something to happen. She had to keep standing, she had to make her ears hear what was being said, and she had to figure out what they were talking about. She had no idea what to do or say. Of course, she had family, but she was not going to call anyone in the middle of the night to…do what? Hold her hand?

"What about family? Does your husband have parents we should notify?" repeated the officer again.

"Oh well…yes," she whispered, "Joseph Small Senior, lives north of Albam."

"Thank you, ma'am, we will contact them," the officer said. He was very polite, even though she could tell that he was terribly nervous by the cracking of his voice and the fact that his hands were shaking. This was a duty that no one ever desired to perform, to inform a wife and family that one of their loved ones had lost their life.

She stood there not knowing what to do. She didn't want to break down in front of these men, strangers who had just informed her that her husband was dead. Actually, she wanted to scream, run away to hide, cry and yell! These strangers who had just informed her of the most horrible unwanted news ever, were standing on her porch looking at her with such pity.

"Ma'am, we are so sorry. Is there anything we can do?" said one of the others who she figured to be a neighbor.

"No." She had her arms wrapped around herself squeezing tighter and tighter to hold herself together, as each moment passed. It seemed to be forever since the time of her dream and now. There was nothing they could do. There was nothing she could do. It is done. She thought there was no one who could help her through this, except Joe, and he was not here. It was, therefore, something she had to endure on her own. She couldn't think or move. Petrified is what they call something that is turned to stone, that cannot move.

"If you are sure you will be all right, we will go," the officer said.

"I can stay if you want me to," the other man spoke. This man she thought to be the preacher of the little church up the road.

"No. Please, I would like to be alone." She thought she had figured out who these men were but, since she and Joe had only purchased this house a few months prior, they had not had time to meet everyone in the small village. The men did not frighten her. She just didn't want them to be with her at this very moment. Tears began to roll down her cheeks. She could not hold them back much longer.

"Are you sure?" he pleaded with her again.

"Yes. Please, I will be alright."

As the men slowly walked away in the dim light of early morning, Yvonne closed the door to the world and sank to the floor.

15

Chapter I

Summer, 1961, school was out for three whole months. Daily routines were beginning to form as they had in previous summers. Vacation Bible School at the church had begun where Yvonne was helping to teach this year. More than a helper, she was actually teaching a class of the young children. This new position of teaching children prompted her to feel more mature, instead of being just one of the students as she had been in years past. She enjoyed working with them, as she was also the busiest babysitter in her little town.

Summer was Yvonne's favorite time of the year. No homework, no worry about what to wear to school each day, no getting up early each morning to catch a bus, and she did not have to think about what the others kids at school thought of her. She could wear shorts, go barefoot, wake up whenever, enjoy the warmth of the sun, and enjoy time with her family.

Each year of her life, summer blossomed with more adventure, experiences, growth, and time to renew her spirit with nature and the outside world. It was free time for her from school, worry, and busy schedules. She could now do things such as swimming, water skiing, biking, slumber parties, be with friends, go on picnics and more. Better yet, this summer, this very day is Yvonne's seventeenth birthday! She was all giddy about turning seventeen. She had finally received her driver's license and now, since she was seventeen, could actually go on a date with a boy, with her parents' permission. Her father had made a rule (it seemed to be made especially for her), that she could not date boys until she reached the age of seventeen. She had not understood this rule he imposed on her for her two older brothers were free to date girls and drive and do things at an age younger than seventeen. The rule had not been an imposition though, because not one boy had ever asked her out so far in her life.

She would sometimes dream about dating, but thought that perhaps she truly was not ready. She had male friendships throughout the years and maybe a crush on a boy or two, but never even got close to a date. There had been many fun times in her life, such as being a cheerleader in junior high for the boys' basketball team, roller skating parties, softball games with the boys and girls in the neighborhood, and mingling with students at school. Yvonne definitely was shy, yet still she had many good relationships with boys as well as girls. After all, she had two older brothers and several cousins who were males. Now that she was seventeen, if and when a boy would ask her for a date, she could reply, "Yes," if she desired to go out with him. Just knowing that she possessed this bit of power gave her a little more attitude and feeling of control of her life. What would she do with that power?

This June day had a special warm feel of the early summer that she welcomed with all her senses. It had been a pleasant, but quiet day so far. Everyone at Bible School had sung 'Happy Birthday' to her as was the common thing to do for one's birthday. Now, her father arrived home from work, the family had dinner together and celebrated her special day with an angel food cake (which her mother had made) with ice cream, and they also sang 'Happy Birthday'. After finishing all that, Yvonne was the first one to be excused from the dinner table and rushed out the door to enjoy the rest of her day to start being seventeen.

She didn't mind that it wasn't a big party or lots of gifts, as most of her birthdays were not. She was delighted to be this wonderful new age. It felt special. There was even a magazine named 'Seventeen'. There must be wonderful things to behold for a seventeen year old girl. Yvonne had no idea what today or tomorrow held for her, but she was excited to explore each moment as a happy seventeen-year-old teen.

Once she stepped outside the house, she climbed on the bicycle to ride around the neighborhood checking out what might be happening on this her special day. She enjoyed riding the bicycle and as the evening cooled, enjoyed the feel of the fresh air as she rode. She wished that her siblings had bicycles so they could all ride together, but the family only possessed one. Riding the bike got her around town faster than walking, although there was no problem with walking. Her family did a lot of walking since they only had one car which her father drove to work every day. Her mother did not have a driver's license, which she never understood, except she didn't have a car to drive anyway.

And then her father had refused permission for Yvonne to get her license when she was only sixteen, which had been a real kick in the gut for her, but he had relented after she had taken the driver's education course in school. Anyway, the bicycle ride seemed to be a good idea for right now. She felt like singing, waving to everyone she passed as though she were in a parade wanting them to notice that she was now seventeen. She pedaled up the hill around the block to where her cousin, Frankie, lived.

She had seen a new boy in town and figured Frankie might know who he is. Her curiosity had been aroused and was very anxious to find out about him. Her cousin was her best friend, around town and at school, often wishing that he were not her cousin so he could be the one to date her. As she approached his yard, she could see several boys gathered around Frankie's car. It was not unusual for them to be at his house since he was one of the few boys to even have a car. It was totally unusual for her to invite herself into a group of boys, but that was what she thought to do.

Normally, she would wave and ride on by. Her heart beat faster. Her second thought was to just ride on by, but somehow she got the courage to stop. She recognized all the boys except one. *Yep, there he was! Wonderful, now what happens? Excitement ran through her body like sun rays on a cloudy day.* She felt numb as she could not believe that she was actually *doing this*.

Her cousin greeted her with a smile, as he always would. "Hey, what's up?" was his casual greeting.

"Nothing," Yvonne replied. "What are you doing?" She said as if she couldn't see who was there or what they were doing. *She did not need to worry though, for her cousin knew her very well and would carry on from here.*

"We are just cleaning the spark plugs on my car. We had a really hard day baling hay for Farmer Allen, so now we are taking it easy," Frankie explained to her as he always would because he knew she understood about cars.

"Really, who all helped to put up the hay?" she asked. Actually, she knew everyone except the new guy, but thought it a good question to find out the new guy's name.

"There was Johnnie, Rich, and Joe Small and me," he replied. "Hey, Joe, meet my cousin, Yvonne."

"Hi," Joe greeted her with an awesome smile.

"Hi" was all Yvonne could speak, as she suddenly became nervous. She was usually not nervous around her cousin or other neighborhood friends, but just meeting this new guy caused her heart to pound. Anyway she had stopped to get the new guy's name, and she had accomplished her mission! This was a whole new ballgame she was playing, and she wasn't sure what the next play should be.

"Joe is staying with his uncle Ray for the summer so he can earn a little cash," Frankie explained further.

"Yes, those bales were heavy though, and I am not use to that hard labor." Joe chuckled. *Was he nervous too? What else could she say?* Feeling awkward, she thought she best move on. She had visions of falling over as she rode away on the bicycle. *Why couldn't she think of something more to say since she was here?*

Johnnie added, "He did pretty well for his first day, should do better tomorrow."

"At least, it wasn't too hot today," she commented lamely.

Then she made her move to get on the bicycle as Frankie cried out, "What's your hurry?" Yvonne was not in a hurry, but all of a sudden her nervousness grew to volcanic proportions. She felt a need to move on.

"See you later," she said as she hopped on the bicycle and coasted on down the hill.

"Right," her cousin called out as he went back toward the car, wondering why all of a sudden she had to leave.

Wow, she thought, *Joe is so cute. I hope I see him again.* She could hardly contain her excitement as she continued on her ride. That was the first time ever she was so bold as to put herself in a situation such as that, but she had wanted to meet the new guy, and it had worked. *Joe Small was his name and now I will never be the same.* She was happy with herself for mustering up the courage to make this huge challenge. Now what could she do? Certainly can't ride around her cousin's house again. Why didn't she stay a little longer and find out more about Joe? Oh well, at least she had made the first move to meet him. Now she would have to wait and see what would transpire next, if anything, with this new guy in her town.

She rode around for a while with the song in her mind: "Seventeen, seventeen, I am seventeen today, so happy and glad to be seventeen." After traveling every street, she ended back at home with a big smile on her face. Her family assumed she was happy about her birthday. She was, but something else had happened on her seventeenth birthday. A day she would never forget. She wrote in her diary: "I met Joe."

As soon as Yvonne had left the group of guys, Joe exclaimed to Frankie, "Wow, man, why haven't you introduced me to her before now?"

Frankie calmly answered, "I have only known you for a couple of days, I must be sure of anyone before I tell them about my cousin, but now you have met her."

"I sure did. Where does she live?"

"Only one block south and one block west. The two-story house on the corner."

"Great, can we go see her after we get done?"

"No, hold your horses. I have to think about it. I don't know if she wants to see you."

"I sure do want to see her again." Joe felt something very good when he met Yvonne. Somehow, she was different than the girls he had known at school. She had a slender body, about his size, a natural look, with no make-up, and a very sweet smile. He wondered if she might like to get to know him. He could hardly wait to see her again.

The boys went back to working on the car. "You need to do this one next," Johnnie said.

"I know," snipped Frankie, "just give me a minute."

"Then what are we going to do next?" asked Rich.

Chapter II

Yvonne had no idea how long she had been sobbing as she sat on the floor against the front door. *What happened to Joe? Why is he gone? I love him and I don't want him to be gone. This just cannot be.* The thoughts kept whirling through her mind on a projector at the end of a reel—flip, flip, flip.

Then she realized she was on the floor in the living room, wondering if the children had heard anything? She checked each bedroom, saw that they were sleeping, went up the stairs to her bedroom, and fell onto the bed. She buried her head in the pillow and sobbed until totally exhausted, dozing off to sleep once again.

Joe had started this new job earlier in the year, which granted them qualification for a loan on this house. The property would be their first home together as a family. It consisted of a few acres in a country setting which was very desirable, with a few neighbors scattered around. Shortly after moving into their home, Yvonne's 33rd birthday was celebrated with Joe, since 1961 when they had first met. It seemed to Yvonne that there were so many lost years since her seventeenth birthday, but now at last they were together.

So far, the year and summer had been good, with adjusting to the new home, Joe's new job, and getting the children settled. Now, it was September, time to get the children back in school. They were pleased to be living back in Illinois, in a new home, having fun with the neighbor children, and enjoying freedom to roam about the neighborhood. For Joe and Yvonne, it seemed that they had really adjusted to life together, and things should only get better with time. Just two days earlier was Joe's 33rd birthday, which had been a small but good celebration for everyone at home.

What happened? Yvonne was startled, as she awoke from her fretful sleep. Thoughts of the awful news she had received earlier, exploded in her head as she became fully conscious. Now, fear consumed her thoughts. She felt lost, lonely, and sick but had to rise to get organized for the day. Finally, as the numbers on the clock became clear, she noticed the daylight becoming brighter. She tried to comprehend how much of what she was thinking was real and how much had been a dream? Then she remembered that it was in her dream that Jesus was knocking on her front door. But then it really wasn't Jesus knocking on the door, it was three men with terrible news about Joe. It wasn't all a dream, it was shockingly very real.

This time yesterday morning Joe prepared for work after six weeks of being incapacitated with a broken ankle. If the doctor released him today, he would possibly be going out on a delivery. Joe was now working for a company, driving a truck which hauled new cars over the states. He had only worked about three months when he jumped off the trailer and broke his ankle. So for a period of time, he had not been able to work until the ankle could heal. Now that he was all better, it was time for him to return to work. He was ready to begin again. He had been a truck driver for over fifteen years, hauling all sorts of commodities over the states. This time his job was a very good paying with benefits. Joe and Yvonne were grateful that he had gained employment with this company, which would provide them with the funds needed to live comfortably as a family.

Yvonne desperately wished that she did not have to get out of bed. She wished it could be yesterday once again when she and Joe had been together. She reviewed the events of yesterday in her mind as to how it had all gone down.

The September morning came forth silently with fresh clean air, birds chirping as they started their flight, with a promise of a very pleasant day. Most of the neighborhood was still sleeping or quietly beginning to rise. Joe was out of bed before daylight. He enjoyed snuggling and sleeping with his wife, but today he was a bit anxious to be off to work after the six week medical layoff. He showered and shaved while Yvonne prepared breakfast for the two of them. He had good thoughts about how his life was evolving lately. Yvonne did an awesome job with the children, the household chores, and giving him the love he so desired. If only he could see his own two children more often. Maybe that would change in the near future. He loved his two children and wished to have more time with them. It was painful for him to think about this situation with his children and often brought him to tears. He didn't know for sure how to change the visitation with them since they lived so far away, but he was going to try.

"Thanks for ironing my shirt," Joe said as he kissed her on the cheek.

"You are welcome," she replied. "Are you hungry?"

"Sure, you know I like to eat." Joe answered as he sat down at the table. They ate their meal in peace and quiet as they smiled at each other. After Joe finished eating, he rose from his chair, "That was delicious, thank you," as he kissed her on the cheek. Joe carried his thermos of coffee and satchel out to the pickup. Yvonne thought that in his excitement to return to work that he was going to leave without kissing her good-bye. As she stood there on the step at the back of the house, he came back to her and with a tight squeeze, gave her a kiss of sweet farewell. "I love you always," Joe said as he starred into her eyes.

"I love you always," Yvonne repeated. She watched him drive away not knowing that this moment would be the last time she would see him alive, and that his kiss would be the last kiss she would ever receive from him. That was twenty-four hours ago.

Today, she was going to wake the children and send them off to school. Yes, she made a quick decision to send them. What would they do at home all day? She was feeling so much loss and pain that she could not bring herself to tell the children just yet about what had happened to Joe. There was no need to have them miss the second day of school. Yvonne had to deal with her thoughts and other details which really were not so much the children's concern, but her own. She did not want them to see her be so vulnerable and lost, which would only upset them. This was the first death which she had to deal with of someone she loved so dearly. Her children had not been exposed to death and the end of life in their short life span. Joe was not their actual father, although they had lived with him almost two years and gotten to know him as their step-father. The impact of Joe's death would not touch them the way it would for her. They might hear about Joe at school, but she was hoping they would not. She needed time to think, time to grieve, and time to reassure that somehow she and the children would be fine. She had been through a lot in her first marriage, since the divorce, and in the short time she was married to Joe, so she needed to get a grip on things before involving the children with so much grief and fear. This situation was a huge explosion to her life that she had not a clue where it would plant her and the children in the near future. She blew her nose again, dried her tears, and went downstairs to start her day as routinely as she possibly could.

The children dressed, ate breakfast, and went out to wait for the bus without fuss or hassle. They were excited about the new school year. As the school bus pulled away, Yvonne thought how grateful she was that school was in session and that it was not still summer when the children would be home all day. She closed the front door as the bus drove away and crashed on the couch with sobs that shook her whole body. Her mind went crazy with worry for tomorrow and trying to figure out what had taken place yesterday after Joe left. *Who would know? How could she find out what had happened? Why did this happen?* She was crying so much, she hardly heard the phone ring the first time. *What time is it? How long had she been on the couch?* Stumbling to the kitchen, she answered the phone, hearing Joe's mother, Millie. How could she talk to her about her son's fatal accident? Yvonne understood how much she loved her first born son, how she had tried to support and help him, and now she had to bear the grief of losing him in such an unexpected way.

"Yvonne, are you okay? Do you know what happened?" Millie queried with a tremor in her voice. Yvonne could hear the pain. How would any mother deal with such a tragedy? Joe's mother had great hopes that at last her son would be happy with this marriage and also with the new job.

"Yes, I am okay," Yvonne replied with a sniff. "I really don't know any more details yet. The deputy said it was an accident of some sort. When they found him, it was too late." She sobbed into the phone. She couldn't believe that she was able to repeat what they had told her. She quickly blew her nose again.

"I thought he was going back to work yesterday," Mrs. Small managed to say. "I talked to him on the phone to wish him happy birthday, he said he was headed back to work in a couple of days. He sounded happy about that."

"Yes he was. I don't know what happened after he left the house." Yvonne wondered herself, wishing she could explain a little further.

"Oh God," she cried, "I just can't believe it. We will meet with you when you are ready to make arrangements."

She managed to say. "I just can't understand and I am too upset to talk anymore."

"All right," was all Yvonne could say as she was thinking that she knew nothing about making arrangements. She had never done anything like that before.

"I'm so sorry, Yvonne. Oh my God. Good bye," she cried as the phone went dead.

"Yes," Yvonne answered, "me too, bye." She hung up the phone and tears exploded again. How was she going to get through this? What could she do, how would she manage, when would she ever be happy again? She just couldn't imagine what was to transpire in her life the next day or two. Thoughts of the accident came to her mind as she tried to imagine how it might have taken place. She just didn't have enough information to figure it out. Did the doctor not release him to go back to work? Was that the reason he was not sent out on a trip with a delivery? Did they perhaps fire him for some unknown reason? How could she find out? Who was going to know the details?

She needed to understand. *Why am I alone again? How am I to manage my life and take care of the children alone?* It was very stressful, confusing, and painful trying to make sense of it all. Walking toward the couch, she flopped down face first again with great sobbing. She didn't know who to call to find out any facts, besides she just didn't want to see anyone right now. Many thoughts ran through her mind over and over until she was exhausted, too exhausted to get dressed or eat or wash dishes or anything! She thought the world could just shut down forever, and she wouldn't care.

Chapter III

Yvonne was happy and excited to have a new person in town and for the fact that he was to her great liking. The young group of teens around town often congregated on the porch of her parents' house in the summer. It was the place to meet to keep in contact with friends throughout the span of summer, to plan a trip to the creek for a swim, or just yik yak about any subject that came up. It was not unusual for two or more kids from the neighborhood to be seen on their front porch. Joe joined the other guys, including Yvonne's cousin, to this group of teens. Yvonne hoped Joe would be coming to see her.

As it turned out, he most certainly did. She felt instant excitement all through her body as she realized how much she was attracted to Joe yesterday and still felt the same today. There were only two times in her young life, so far, when she had truly been attracted to someone else. The first person she liked was a classmate in first grade, whom she liked very much and considered him her special friend. When her family moved to the country and she did not see him anymore, she wrote him letters for a year or so trying to keep in touch with this special person.

The second attraction happened just last year, when a fourth generation cousin had come to visit her family. Charles was her age and they bonded instantly. The connection was sweet and swift. Although they had very little time together, they enjoyed the interaction of getting to know each other. Sitting by each other in the car, playing tag, and laughing a lot, was all they shared. She saw him only one more time as her family passed through the suburbs of Chicago on a family vacation.

Her father stopped to visit their family, which turned into a lovely visit, one that she would always remember. That was the last time she ever saw him or heard from him. Those were very short interludes of friendship with a person whom you cared for so much. Now this was the third time in her life, when she was very much attracted to someone of the opposite sex.

"Hi cousin, hi Joe, everybody," she tried to be calm as she greeted the approaching boys, but the thrill she felt inside was almost too much to contain. The smile on her face showed how excited she was.

She heard Joe's voice as greetings were announced. "Hi, Yvonne, how are you doing today?"

"I am just fine. Did you guys put up hay again, today?"

Joe's replied without hesitation, "We sure did, and I have had about enough of that hard work."

Yvonne understood that it was a hard job, but she thought Joe had come to the country for the purpose of working, and he shouldn't even think about quitting so soon. Sometimes one had to do hard task because the job needs to be done. Every summer the farmers would cut the alfalfa, timothy, or grass when it was tall enough, then he would rake it into rows and let it dry before it was baled. The farmer would always hire several boys on baling day to load the bales onto a wagon and then unload them in the barn to be stored for further use. This chore was a hard task lasting a day or two depending on the amount of hay to be baled. The farmer paid the boys for their help and fed them lunch on the days they worked for him. It was good experience for the boys, physically and financially. Yvonne's brothers had done the task many times.

Frankie spoke, "It was so hot today that we were soaked with sweat and covered with dirt and hay from head to toe. We couldn't wait to sit down in the shade to cool off and have a drink."

Joe added his comment, "For sure, I thought I might pass out before we got to sit."

Yvonne did feel a little sorry for the guys, but at least they got paid for their efforts. "I'm glad you all survived, it really was hot today," she relented, trying to ease their misery.

Yvonne's sisters were always involved with the group gathering on the porch. In fact, she and her sisters were almost always together sharing friends, chores, and activities. As Yvonne was the older sister in the family, she was sort of responsible for all of them (her sisters that is). They were very close, although each one was slightly different in their thoughts, actions, and physical capabilities. Elaine was always trying to be the boss, yet some did not care to go her way. Doris was more friendly, funny, cooperative, and willing to do whatever the group chose to do.

This group of sisters, cousins, and friends just weren't likely to keep anyone from being part of the fun they might be able to share. Tonight they talked mostly about what they did last summer, what happened in school last year, and about some of the friends who were not present. They talked about going swimming, celebrating the 4th of July, and about movies that they would like to see. Johnnie would tell a funny story and all laughed. Then another story would be told and everyone laughed. No one stood back in the corner being shy or silent. The summer nights on the porch were enjoyed by all in attendance, especially this year for Yvonne since she turned seventeen. She wrote in her diary of Joe coming to see her!

Now, this little village of Old Ripley was hardly a half-mile long in length down the main street. A grocery store was on the north end and a tavern on the south. The one and only church sat almost one block south of Yvonne's house. There was also a street west of the main road and one shorter street to the east of Main Street. The Burch house stood on the corner, in the middle of town, on the main street. It was a convenient gathering place and where the most children of the village resided, in one household. Her brothers often had friends who came to visit also, or her brothers might sometimes be gone.

At this time in her life, both brothers had been away serving time in the military services. One had been in the Air Force in Virginia, and the other in the Navy in California. She missed her brothers a lot whenever they were away from home. Only recently, her eldest brother had married and returned to the village to live as their neighbor, which was nice. Yvonne's school mates were the children of the grocery store owner, the tavern owner, the farmers, and of the other people who lived in the village. It was a great place to live, as far as she was concerned.

Grandma lived on the other end of the block, so she got to see her daily. Other relatives lived close also. Everyone knew everybody, as all the children walked or pedaled bikes around the town. Neighbors greeted each other when they met, looked out for each other, and for a small rural community, it was tops.

The next night, only Frankie and Joe came to Yvonne's house. Yvonne was happy to see them and hurried out the front door to greet them. She still felt a little nervous that she might mess up this new friendship, which she very much wanted to keep it going. Frankie could see how she liked Joe, so he guided the two of them in conversation as best he could, to please his favorite cousin, Yvonne.

"Hi, Yvonne," they greeted in chorus.

"Hi," she replied smiling. "What's up?"

"We just came over to chat a bit. Is that alright?" asked Joe.

"Great," she answered as they each took a seat on the porch bench. "So how do you like it in our little village?" Yvonne began asking Joe.

"It is certainly different than where I live in the city. This farm work is hard for me, but I guess I will survive," he replied as they both laughed.

"So what else can you tell us about yourself?" she asked Joe.

"There is nothing great to tell," Joe commenced, and then proceeded to talk more about his life up to now. "I don't do very well in any subject at school. I lost my driver's license three months after getting them because of drinking with some friends. My parents are not happy with me.”

Yvonne was sorry to hear this because she did not drink or believe that teens should try to indulge in the habit of drinking or smoking either. She was familiar with the results of drinking because her parents, aunts, uncles, and even her older brother would sometimes drink. There were times in her life when episodes concerning family members drinking, had even embarrassed her in front of one of her friends. She wanted no part of alcohol in her life, thinking that she found life far too interesting to blur it with the effects of alcohol. She hoped Joe had learned his lesson about drinking and driving and would be the wiser for it. She quickly decided to overlook this past little mistake and hoped it would not be an issue with them.

Yvonne picked up the conversation, “I like going to school, playing in the band, and participating in the girls’ sports activities.” Joe listened to her, but when she paused to allow him to speak, he did not have anything further to comment about his time at school.

“Hmmmm.” She wondered how their relationship might progress with those facts; she very much enjoyed school, while he did not, he had tried drinking which she never would, he had already lost his driver’s license, while she had just gotten hers. But she wasn’t ready to write him off yet. She mentally shoved these facts to the back of her mind so they would not interfere with the progress of this new relationship. Joe was so very cute in her eyes, intriguing with his every move and every word. She was able to talk to him with an ease she had never felt before with anyone. This was definitely part of the whole attraction, that she felt very comfortable around Joe.

At other times when she even thought of some boy as a 'boyfriend', she would enter panic mode, clam up, and basically become a statue. With Joe, she didn't feel the shyness overwhelming her, nor would she reject any chance to see him. Even though she had only known him a few days, she felt pretty sure that she wanted to get to know him better. The three of them sat on the porch for a long time that evening, chatting like old friends. After some time, Frankie commented, "I think I'll just head on down the road."

"Oh no, please don't go," pleaded Yvonne.

"Don't rush off, man," Joe added. "We like having you with us." So he stayed and all three enjoyed the evening for a while longer. They finally said good night and Yvonne watched as the two boys walked on down the road.

The next morning, Yvonne attended Vacation Bible School enjoying time with her young students, even though they challenged her authority every minute. Later in the afternoon, she gathered her sisters and other neighborhood friends to play a game of softball. The guys were able to join since they had not baled hay during the day. Playing softball was one of the activities they all enjoyed. Joe's attendance at this time was certainly welcomed. Yvonne was pleased every time he arrived with the other guys. After the game, she and Joe and her sisters walked all through the village, talking and laughing about how Yvonne had gotten a home run, how Joe struck out, and what a fun time everyone had. They chatted on about Halloween tricks, some vacation trip, or a funny thing that happened at school.

Walking up and down the main street until it was quite late and time to turn in. They all sounded off their "Good nights" and departed.

The neighborhood gatherings and activities continued most days, only the activity varied. On one day, Joe and Yvonne sat out in the swing in the yard telling jokes and laughing about the simplest detail of the funny story. This was the first time Joe mustered the courage to come to her house without any of the other guys. He came just to see her. When this happened, she realized he wanted to be with her. Joe's attention toward her brought happiness and gave her a special good feeling. She looked forward to each day hoping she would see him again. She never had to go look for him, he always showed. Yvonne's sisters and others of the group noticed how much Joe and Yvonne were attracted to each other. Her cousin was happy for her. Now if only he could find someone who would be just like Yvonne, he too would be happy.

One particular night the next week, after a couple of hours visiting on the porch, the boys decided it best that they leave the house before Yvonne's mother ran them off. She wouldn't do that unless one of them became unruly or quite boisterous. Since it was a weekday though, the group knew they needed to be quiet around the house because her father went to bed early, so he could rise early for work the next day. Yvonne's parents were fairly lenient with the children, allowing them to enjoy their youthful days, especially in the summer when there was no school. Yvonne didn't want the boys to leave just yet, but thought it considerate of them to think of her father. *Was that the real reason they were leaving?*

Joe commented to her before he left, "Mom is picking me up tomorrow to take me home for a few days. I don't want to leave, but she said that auntie needed a break from me, so I have to go. I will return as soon as I can, and I will miss you."

Yvonne was a little disappointed to hear that he would be gone, but understood. She cooed a little 'miss you too'. And then spoke louder, "Bye, Joe, bye Frankie, see you later," as she watched them walk away. She wrote in her diary of the happy feelings.

"Goodnight," they hollered and waved.

Joe gave Frankie a pat on the back as they walked. "You have a sweet cousin."

"I know," replied Frankie. "Don't ever forget that she is my cousin, and always be good to her."

"Yes, sir, I will, I will do that." Joe had every intention of getting to know Yvonne very well. He intended to be very nice to her. His heart beat with a soft, good, easy beat as he thought about her. Plans began to race in his mind as to the near future. Joe asked Frankie more questions about Yvonne. Did she have many boyfriends? Well, why not? He was pleased with all he was learning. Joe felt very lucky to have come to this town, to meet a group of guys to be friends with, and to meet someone like Yvonne.

Helping with Bible school filled each morning, and band practice on Monday evenings, also on her schedule, took up part of that evening. She liked playing in the Municipal Band for the summer, for which she received payment for each practice and each concert in which she performed. Practice was held on Monday evenings and the concerts were performed on the following Wednesday evening at the park. Yvonne planned to attend every practice and concert for the summer. She also helped around the house, keeping her room clean, washing dishes, cooking an occasional meal, and learning to sew. When Joe was gone, she wished he hadn't left, but realized that he needed to spend time with his family. Besides, she did have other things to do. Yvonne had a couple of friends with whom she usually spent time with. Last year she did a lot with her friends, staying overnight, going to a movie, or bike rides. She still saw them at church or band, but whenever she had a chance to be with Joe, she chose him. Her life had not changed a lot, but yet it had.

When Joe arrived once again at her house the next week, Yvonne nearly knocked her sister over trying to get out the front door. He started out with a question as she greeted him on the porch, "Will you come to dinner at Uncle Ray's tomorrow night?" He had that sweet smile on his face.

"Yes, I can come," Yvonne replied. She knew Joe's aunt and uncle because she had babysat several times with their children. It was just a little awkward thinking about eating with the family and Joe, but she wanted to go because Joe had asked.

"Great," Joe burst out. "I will walk up to meet you when it is time."

"Okay," Yvonne replied. "How was your time at home?"

"Pretty boring, I couldn't wait to get back out here. I missed you, that is for sure."

Yvonne felt a blush come over her face. Joe saw her blush and with a chuckle as he said, "I really did."

During dinner the next night at Joe's uncle Ray's, it was hard to have a conversation, as the children all smiled at her, and Joe's uncle teased them both. She was nervous and could hardly eat. Yvonne knew Joe's uncle would tease them, while his Aunt Sue was pleasantly warning Yvonne not to pay any attention to Ray. After dinner, Joe and Yvonne sat in the living room with everyone for a while to be sociable. This, too, was nerve racking for Yvonne. She could always talk to the kids and play with them when she was baby-sitting, but tonight, she couldn't think of anything to say. Finally, Joe and Yvonne were able to say their thanks for everything and quickly slipped out the door for a quiet walk home. Holding hands as they walked, Joe began talking with a bit of a stutter," I sure do like being with you. Would you be my girl?"

"Yes, Joe, I would," she replied. She was seventeen and ready for a boyfriend. She squeezed his hand tighter and smiled. They walked on up the street to her house as a very happy couple. She was so glad that she had taken a bike ride up to her cousin's house on her birthday. Now she was Joe's girlfriend! She wrote about this day in her diary!

Joe, too, was extremely happy about meeting Yvonne and desperately wanted her to be his steady girl. It was hardly even two weeks since they had met. Was it too soon to have these good feelings? He didn't care how short a time it had been, he felt good being with her. He thought they made a good matching pair with their size being about the same, they both had dark hair, and their characteristics were similar. Yvonne was about five foot three and one hundred pounds, Joe was the same height and maybe one hundred thirty pounds. She had short auburn hair, while Joe's was black and wavy. Joe and Yvonne were able to be themselves while they were with each other, with no pretense at all. Yvonne had made a good impression on Joe. She was influencing his attitude and behavior. He liked her and was very willing to change however he needed to.

Each day was always too short but always fun. Once again at the end of the week, Joe's mother came out to visit her sister and check up on Joe. She confronted Joe that probably he should go back home, especially if he wasn't doing any work for any farmers. She thought it was too much of a burden on her sister to take care of Joe besides her own children. Joe wanted to stay longer, but then he had a great idea. "Mom, could Yvonne visit with us for the week-end?"

She replied, "Well, yes if it is permissible with her parents." So Joe quickly went to Yvonne's house to ask her mother if she could go visit at Joe's house. Much to Yvonne's surprise, her mother said, "Yes." *So now, what situation did Yvonne get into? Yvonne thought her mother would say 'no' and that would be the end of that, but much to her surprise she said, "Yes." Yvonne packed an overnight bag and left with Joe and his* mother. As she rode along in the car, she became worried about this decision to go to Joe's house. *What would she do while there? How would she be with Joe 24/7 without being so dull or so backward?* Thinking about this new situation in which she was suddenly involved, brought many new questions to her which she had never even considered before. Evidently, her mother thought she was old enough to make good decisions and be responsible. Yvonne was not so sure of herself at the moment, maybe this had been a hasty decision, made without much thought. Well she would just have to make the best of it. The shyness began to overcome her, making it difficult to act natural or to be friendly with Joe's family. Joe's mother was great as she seemed to understand what was happening with her son and the new girl in his life. It was harder to face Joe's dad when he arrived home after a hard day at work, as Yvonne had no idea what to say to him. He seemed cranky, difficult to talk to. Yvonne simply said, "hi" and blushed quite profusely. Joe chuckled as he took her hand to lead her out into the yard. Yvonne could easily deal with Joe's younger sisters, as she was an excellent babysitter and could handle most situations with children. She tried to be casual that first afternoon at Joe's house, but it seems that she failed. Anyway, this was her first time to visit a boyfriend's family, what could one expect? She really had no idea what to do, what Joe expected, or what his mother and father were thinking.

Joe was delighted as a hummingbird in a fresh garden of flowers, as he tried to entertain his new guest. Yvonne was standing in the yard close to Joe, when he suggested to his sister, "Take a picture of us." Joe reached his arm around her waist as his sister snapped the picture. The feel of his arm sent chills all through her and the warmth of his body against her as they stood there in the sun caused her to blush. This exciting moment of her seventeenth year registered with her as another memory never to be forgotten. She managed to get through the rest of the evening by sticking close to Joe and not saying much besides 'yes, or no' to any question asked of her. She realized how shy she was acting but could not seem to overcome it. Joe was very happy and pleasant the whole day, smiling at her and teasing her about being so shy.

The Small's home was newer and nicer than her home. It was white with a large front porch all the way across the front of the house with a two foot wall surrounding and two large pillars at the top of the steps that ran down to the sidewalk out front. There was a swing big enough for three people to sit in, and room enough on the porch for many friends to visit. How cool! Yvonne thought that this porch would be much more accommodating for friends than the porch at her house. Joe's house was a two-story with only his bedroom upstairs. It was a fairly large room with all his possessions arranged nicely. Her house was an old two-story which was built in the late 1880s. There were four bedrooms upstairs where her bedroom was, but it was not as nice as Joe's. Her house sat on the corner of the street of a very old village without much traffic. Joe's house also sat on the corner, but the street out front was quite a busy one since it was a main road coming out of the town. She liked their more modern house very much and secretly wished it was the one she could live in. Besides the lovely house, she liked the way Joe's mother accepted her and tried to help her feel comfortable. Yvonne would be sleeping on the couch, which was fine with her.

The next day was a very nice as far as the weather, so she and Joe decided to walk to the shopping mall just to occupy their time. Joe's two sisters walked with them which was fine with Yvonne because she was use to her own sisters tagging along. It was a pleasant, happy walk holding hands, smiling, laughing as they went. When they finished looking around in the small store, they bought a soda to share, and then with the thought of returning home, Joe began to complain, "You know it is kind of far to walk, so I'll call Mom to come pick us up."

Yvonne chided him, "No, don't call her, we can walk." So they walked the whole six blocks back to the house. Yes, he liked her. Yes, she thought he was all right. Spending the day with Joe and his sisters turned out to be quite pleasurable. She helped Joe's younger sister to roller skate, and helped the other one to braid a bracelet of yarn. Today she was able to relax a little more and feel comfortable with Joe's family.

After the evening meal was finished, Mrs. Small drove the two of them uptown to the movie theatre. For the first time, Yvonne thought that she was actually on a date. They sat through the movie sharing popcorn and holding hands. Joe even put his arm around her shoulders which seemed most appropriate since they were on a date. Yvonne was so enthralled with the fact that she was with a guy at a movie that she hardly noticed what was happening on the screen, or what the movie was about. Happiness was building inside her, which she did not know how to handle. His mother picked them up when the movie was over taking them back to the house. They sat out on the porch swing for a while enjoying the togetherness. Then Joe leaned toward her kissing her on the forehead and then on the lips. It was a sweet gesture on Joe's part, a compliment for Yvonne, and a marvelous ending for her first date with Joe.

Chapter IV

Yvonne was feeling totally exhausted, even though she hadn't done anything all day. Lying on the couch, she heard a car pull into the drive. At least, she thought she heard a car in between shedding tears and perhaps sleeping a little. She blew her nose, brushed her hair out of her face, slowly walked to the door looking like a scare crow that had been blowing in the wind all night. She saw the Reverend Henry walking upon the porch. Yvonne could not believe her own eyes. This man had come especially to see her! She quickly opened the door to allow him entrance. He stepped forward to greet her and immediately wrapped his arms around her warming her body and soul. Yvonne smiled with tears in her eyes, pain in her heart, and joy to see this man whom she had come to love and respect.

"It is so good to see you. Thanks for coming." She cried as they hugged.

"I am so sorry to hear about Joe," he began. "I just had to make the trip down here to see you. Please, relax, lie down if you want. I'll sit here on the floor so we can talk." He took her hand as he sat beside the couch. It felt very weird to be horizontal while the preacher sat on the floor beside her. Yet, it calmed her for him to be with her at this time.

"I know this has to be a very difficult time for you, Yvonne. You must have faith that God is watching over you and will see you through." He paused as he patted her hand. "Losing a loved one is a hard situation to deal with. God is with you and will provide a path for you." He was silent a moment just sitting there holding her hand. Then he asked, "How are the children? Tell me all about the past year."

She sniffed, blew her nose, and tried to think where to start with her story, her past, her heart break." I will start back where I last saw you. We were very happy to be married, but had to make some important and quick decisions about where to live and how to provide for us as a family. Joe wanted to move to California, so we did. My brother was a big help to us. Some days were very good, as one would expect, but there were a lot of adjustments to make." He nodded his head as she spoke. She knew he understood what had to take place in a second marriage. He knew the fear, pain, and sorrow of death. Being a minister, he had counseled people through such tragedies and preached at many funerals. He understood the love and happiness in her life to have been reunited with Joe. He understood her loss right now of losing Joe after being married to him for less than two years. He listened and nodded in response to every word she spoke. He waited patiently as she wiped the tears and regained her composer once again.

She continued, "Joe tried very hard to make it work, and I guess it was working, we just all got kind of home sick and decided to come back to Illinois. It took time to find a house and work here, but we got that established, and then…" She broke down and cried again.

"I know, I know," he said as he nodded. "It's going to be better."

"You know we loved each other, but all the changes we made so quickly, everything that had developed in each of us, plus involving the children with this new relationship was a big challenge." She struggled with each word.

"I know what you are saying," he squeezed her hand. "I think probably you were doing as well as possible."

She shook her head in doubt. He said, "Yes, you are."

He stayed with her for a couple of hours, which comforted her immensely. His words of concern for her and the children were genuine. Then he prayed, "Heavenly Father, I come to You at this moment to ask You to be with this young mother. Lord, please comfort her and strengthen her today and in the troubling days to follow. Strengthen her faith in You during this very difficult time. She is one of Your special children, who loves You and believes You are her God. Thank you for your continuing grace, compassion, strength, and love. In Jesus' name I pray, Amen."

"I'm sorry that I have to get back home. I'm truly sorry about Joe, and I pray that God remains with you and will give you strength to live as best as you can in the days to come," he said after he stood up.

Tears kept rolling down her cheeks because she could not stop them. She stood up, hugged him once again. "Thank you so much for the visit and comforting words. I value your friendship." She truly did not want him to leave for his presence brought her such comfort.

"Please call me if I can help out." He told her as he walked to the door.

"I just don't know where I am headed right now," she whimpered.

"God will help you figure it out," he assured her.

She respected him, thought him to be a wonderful, sincere man who understood her quite well. She waved to him as he drove away.

Before she had time to freshen up, the school bus pulled to a stop in front of the house. The children popped out of the bus like frogs from a cage. *What should she say to them? How will they react?* Excited from their first day of school, the children hustled into the house bursting with their information. "Mom, Gary said Joe was killed last night. Is that true?" Dolly asked. The other children also looking at their mom with much worry on their faces, waited for her response.

"Yes, that is true. Joe wrecked his pickup and died," Yvonne said solemnly as she tried to be strong.

"Why did he do that?" Dolly continued. "Will we have to move again? What about Joe's children?"

"His children are with their mother. They will be very sad. I think maybe we will not move again. We will have to wait and see. I don't know how Joe had a wreck." Yvonne answered as best she could. She hugged them as they sat beside her on the couch. "I will take care of you as before." She almost broke down and cried, but she tried hard not to as a tear rolled down her cheek.

"Why did Joe wreck his truck?" Jesse repeated. Sissy and little Jacob said nothing, but had much wonder in their eyes.

"Well, I'm not sure what happened, he, well, just that somehow he ran off the road and crashed." She could not come up with any more explanation.

"Oh well, he should have been more careful," replied Jesse.

"Yes, Jesse, that is right. We always need to be more careful," Yvonne answered. They all sat there in the living room in silence for a moment, then Yvonne said, "I am very sad about Joe, as you can see, but understand that I will still be here for you all. There is nothing that will separate us or nothing that will hurt us. Do you understand?" They looked at her with worry in their eyes as they answered in unison, "Yes." Then she asked, "What do you think we should have for supper?"

Jesse said, "I want spaghetti."

Dolly voiced her opinion, "I vote for tacos." It was then Yvonne realized how hungry she was and that she had not eaten anything all day. It was difficult for her to think or do even the simplest of chores. She whispered a prayer as she headed toward the kitchen, "I need to get through this, God please help me."

The children did their homework, ate their supper, played outside with the neighbor children until it was time for bed. As each one asked a question, Yvonne tried to comfort them with words of strength, more for herself than them, and to prepare them for the next few days. It was very hard to find the words which would actually assure her also. She managed the best she knew, only was not able to complete all tasks at hand. Piling the dishes in the sink, helping Jacob prepare for bed, and picking up dirty clothes, she realized that a day had ended. Not a normal day for sure, but the first full day without Joe, a lonely day of many to come.

She trudged up the stairs to her bedroom, which had been a wonderful place for her private time with Joe. It would be the place in which she still felt the closest to him when she was in it. Sleeping alone wasn't unusual since Joe was gone on the truck for his work, but just knowing that he would never sleep with her again caused the tears to well up over, and over again. When Joe was home, she went to sleep with her head on his shoulder as his arm surrounded her. She enjoyed the smell and warmth of his body next to her. After making love, they always slept very well together, snuggling the whole night through. Many nights were shared this way since they had married. Suddenly, the dream she had last night came to her mind. This dream mystified her because it seemed so real that she could see Jesus knocking at her front door just like a picture that she had seen. Was the dream a sign, a warning? She accepted it as a comforting sign from God. She prayed, "Please be with Joe and please help me get through the rest of my days."

Morning arrived as the sun shined brightly through the east window of her bedroom. This day could have been so different from what was about to transpire. Joe could have been here to kiss her 'good morning', but not today. This day, she had to get the kids ready for school, and then get herself to the meeting with the funeral director to make arrangements for Joe's funeral. Yvonne had not a clue what all the plans would involve. She was scared. Her only hope to having things go well, was that Joe's family would be there to help her with all the information. Everyone, including Yvonne, was still very curious as to what caused the accident. Eventually, Yvonne did collect more information such as; Joe was out drinking most of the afternoon and night. Someone said perhaps he had turned quickly trying to avoid hitting a deer or he might have been driving too fast and swerved off the road. She didn't know what to believe for he was an excellent driver. How would she ever retrieve the correct information?

The children were very cooperative through their morning routine. Yvonne was thankful that they were exceptionally quiet, realizing that they were having trouble comprehending what was happening especially since their mother was so sad. "I will pick you up after school instead of you riding the bus home. Please do not worry about things and try to have a good day," were her final instructions to them as they walked out the door.

As soon as the children boarded the bus, she wilted on the couch. Tears ran down her cheeks as thoughts ran through her mind over and over. How would she get her strength and courage up for the day to get through this meeting at the funeral home, and just how would she continue her life without Joe? She sat on the couch for some time trying to gather momentum to move. She did her best to focus on today's schedule, stood up venturing to the bathroom, took a hot shower, dressed, and was able to drive the ten miles to the funeral home.

Joe's family was all waiting outside the large two story building when she arrived. Pleased to see that all of them had come, she hugged each one as the tears fell. They waited a moment then Mrs. Small asked again the question everyone wanted to know, "Do you know what happened?"

"Only what the police have told me," she stammered as she blew her nose.

Joe's mother continued, "I thought he was going back to work. When I wished him a happy birthday, he told me he was ready to start working again. He really sounded enthused."

"Yes, I know." Yvonne replied. "He did go first to see the doctor to be released and hopefully, on with a delivery, but I don't know what happened. He never called me to say what was up."

The funeral director came to the door and invited all to come in. After everyone sat down in one room, he began to ask the necessary questions for pertinent information. All were quietly looking at Yvonne. She answered each question as best she could often glancing toward Millie to see if she had any further information. Some answers Yvonne did not know and allowed her mother-in-law to fill them in. Where would the burial be? Yvonne had no idea. Thankfully Joe's parents had purchased a few lots in a cemetery close to where they lived. Joe would be buried there. Yvonne would choose a nice suit for him to wear. Now, came the hardest part when they had to select a casket. Tears rolled down her cheeks as well as his mother's and sister's. Holding hands they followed the man in charge, looking at too many caskets. All were nice. Eventually they agreed on a very nice dark wood. Flowers were ordered as well as music choices and a minister to speak at the memorial. That completed the arrangements. Everyone was emotionally drained, especially Yvonne and Mrs. Small. They each hugged and cried as departure separated them.

Yvonne felt as she had been through a tornado, and wished she could just be at home relaxing with Joe. She thought it would be nice to have Joe hold her again and let all the fear melt away from her shaking, weak, body. She sat in the car for a moment to gain her composer before driving to the school to pick up the children. More questions surfaced in her mind; *how would all this funeral expense be paid for? What would the insurance cover? Who would take care of this stuff and when? She knew there would be insurance benefits, but how much or to whom it would be paid, she knew not.*

The children were glad to see their mother as they approached the car. They needed to see that she would still be there for them. She had not realized it before, but now she saw in their young faces, the worry. "Hi my little sweeties," she said trying to smile.

"Hi Mommy," each one answered as they entered the car.

Yvonne needed something to wear to the service, although she didn't feel like shopping. Going to the nearest store, she looked for something suitable. Trying on a few dresses, she was amazed how everything her normal size was hanging loosely on her body. It was then she realized that she had lost several pounds in just a couple days! Well, she thought it only stands to reason because she hadn't eaten hardly anything, but thought it must be the emotional stress that had the most effect on her weight in such a short time. Finally she found a skirt and vest that would do, quickly made her purchase, and headed home to prepare supper for the children. They were being so patient, so good. She knew she was blessed to have such wonderful children.

The telephone was ringing as they entered the house. Yvonne hurried to answer before the caller might hang up. It was Yvonne's brother from California calling to express his condolences. "Hi Sis," he began.

"Hello, Daryl, thanks for calling," she croaked.

"Mom called to tell me about Joe, I am so sorry," he expressed to her his sympathy. He knew how difficult her life had been for years. He wished she could have had a better, easier life.

"I'm so lost and scared," she cried. "I don't know what I am going to do."

"It will be alright, Sis. You will get through this because you need to for the children. You know you will receive social security benefits for you and each of the children." Yvonne was surprised to hear that. She thought that Joe's children would receive benefits, but didn't expect to get them for her children.

"No, I did not know that," she replied.

"Yes you will. If you don't hear from the social security office, call them to apply." He told her. "Be sure to check on it. Okay? I'm sorry I can't be there, but I am thinking about you always."

"Thanks Daryl, for all you have done for me." He was the one who helped them to get settled in California. He made arrangements for Joe with his work, and assisted them as they looked for a place to live. She felt totally indebted to him for all he had provided for her previously. He had always been guidance for her throughout her life.

"That's okay, I understand. I love you, Sis, and want the best for you. Bye, I will talk to you again soon." He hung up.

She was not ready to say good bye to him. She wanted to hear his voice, some more words of comfort, most of all to have him be with her. His was so good to her. She cried but felt a little better hearing the news that he spoke of. It gave her some hope as far as finances in the near future.

Somehow in a haze, she prepared a meal. The children consumed their food quietly, as no one knew what to say. The dishes were piling up in the sink, the laundry pile was growing, but all Yvonne wanted to do was lie down and cry. That would not be a good thing to do in front of the children, so she stayed calm and dried eyed until they were in bed, then the tears rolled down her cheeks. All the questions of today and worries of tomorrow were racing in her mind. Amid the sniffles and sobs, she noticed a car pull into the drive. Wondering who could be arriving at this time of night, she opened the door.

"Oh my goodness," she cried. "What a nice surprise." It was Yvonne's ex-sister-in-law. *What a comforting moment! How did she know? Why did she come? Yvonne was so excited and happy to see her. It was a* great relief to have someone to be with at this moment. They had not seen each other for over two years.

"This is wonderful!" exclaimed Yvonne as they hugged and cried. "Jean, I am so thrilled to see you. How did you know? Why did you come at this time of the night?"

"I just decided that you might need someone to talk to, so here I am," she responded. "Is it okay with you that I am here?"

"You bet it is. Thanks so much." They hugged and held onto each other as they entered the house. "Jean, I am just so overcome with grief and worry, I'm not sure what to think, or say, or do."

Jean replied, "It is going to be alright. You just hang in there."

Yvonne and Jean sat in the kitchen talking about the children, the accident, her own physical and mental well-being, and how unsure she felt about what to do in this situation. Once again she unfolded the events of her life of the last two years. The ex-family's relationship was greatly strained since the divorce of the children's father. Not having contact with any of them had been sad and stressful. She didn't know what they knew or thought of her.

Jean commented, "Yvonne, you are strong enough and can make all your tomorrows a better day," as she walked toward the sink.

"Oh Jean, no I'm sorry that I am such a mess," cried Yvonne. "Don't be washing my dishes."

Jean replied, "I came to help, so you just sit and talk to me. I can do these dishes while I listen."

Relief flooded over Yvonne. She was absolutely glad that Jean had shown up tonight. Jean quickly washed all the dishes as they conversed about family and days gone by. Jean was able to offer Yvonne some much needed compassion. The evening passed, and Jean said, "I suppose I best get home."

Yvonne didn't want her to leave just yet, but understood why she would need to go home to her family. "Thank you for coming, Jean." Yvonne hugged her tightly. "You don't know how much this means to me. I really needed someone tonight. I'm glad it was you."

Jean smiled as she spoke, "I debated on coming, now I'm glad I did."

"Thanks ever so much, goodnight." Yvonne walked into the house after watching Jean drive away. She felt totally exhausted and could hardly wait to climb into her bed even though it reminded her that Joe was not home or ever will be.

As she lay in bed thinking about the day, the tears slowly trickled down her cheeks as she reminisced about yesterday and the day before. She knew that Joe was gone on a forever trip never to return, but still the reality of it all was hard to comprehend. She reflected on a bit more information that that she had received about Joe, which was that: he had reported to the doctor, who had given him a release to go back to work the following day. So, why hadn't Joe come back home or at least why had he not called her? Joe was always good about using the telephone. This time, he did not. So what else had transpired that day? She tossed and turned for more than an hour, just thinking and crying, until through exhaustion, she fell asleep, lonely, confused, and lost.

Chapter V

Going to a drive-in movie was a special treat in summer time. Yvonne didn't get to go often, but occasionally her brothers or cousin would go and take her and her sisters. It was great to watch the movie on the huge screen in the outdoors. One could see all the other people sitting in their cars or on lawn chairs or blankets on the ground. Looking up, the stars and moon became the ceiling. This time was a very special summer night that Joe and Yvonne got to go to a drive-in movie with her brother, Edward and his wife, Carla. Ed had stopped by the house the night before on his way home from work to inform Yvonne of a generous offer. He said, "If you get your sister to babysit my little ones, you and Joe can go to the drive-in with Carla and me."

"Really?" she exclaimed. "Sure, I'll get one of them to babysit. Thanks." She ran into the kitchen to find her sister. "Doris, will you babysit for Edward's kids tomorrow night?" she asked almost out of breath. Yvonne appreciated the invitation from her brother since neither she nor Joe had a car to go anywhere themselves. The drive-in was a place she loved to visit in the summer.

"Well, I would like to go too," Doris answered.

"Not this time, Sis. Ed is taking Joe and me. So, please, will you?"

"Oh, I see! I guess I will," she answered as she walked out the door.

"Good! Thanks, you are great."

This summer was progressing very differently from previous ones. Last year was all right, but Yvonne didn't have a boyfriend and was not doing any of the activities she had done so far this summer, since her birthday. Often Yvonne would babysit for her brother while he and his wife went to the movie, but this time her sister would do the babysitting so she and Joe could go join them.

The young couple was ready and waiting on the front porch when her brother stopped in front of the house. "Hi, Ed, hi Carla," she almost sang as she climbed into the back seat of her brother's car with Joe right behind her. "Thanks for taking us tonight," she continued.

"Yes, thanks," Joe joined in with a big smile. Edward smiled too as he drove away. For Yvonne, it was cool to be on a double date with her big brother, holding Joe's hand and smiling. Edward probably felt more like he was babysitting his sister, because for many years when she was very little, he did take care of her. Now, she was growing up but would always be his little sister.

Carla spoke, "I'm excited to see this movie, and happy you two could join us. I'm glad Doris is babysitting. Joe, have you been to this drive-in?"

"Not this one, but I like to go to the one at home when I can."

The evening was nice, not too hot, as they settled at dusk to watch the movie. As much as Yvonne enjoyed going to see any movie, it was hard to concentrate. Her brother and sister-in-law sitting in the front seat could easily turn around to see her and Joe sitting so close. Nothing wrong with that, still she was conscience that they might look. How exciting! Joe hardly let go of her hand except to eat some popcorn.

It was a quiet drive home. Joe and Yvonne exited the car in front of the house. Joe shook hands with Ed and said, "Thank you again for the ride, the movie, and for being so nice." Yvonne hugged her brother. He knew how grateful she was.

"You both are welcome, don't stay up too late." He said with a big smile.

Carla waved and said, "See you tomorrow."

"Thanks," Yvonne replied. Neither Joe nor Yvonne was ready for the night to end, even though it was late. They walked out to the swing in the yard and sat there enjoying the coolness of the night, and the beauty of the stars, neither speaking. It was enjoyable sitting next to each other. Yvonne wished that every day could continue just like this one. Finally Joe whispered, "Good night, I love you," gently kissing her before he walked down the street to his uncle's house. Yvonne watched him walk away into the dark until she could see him no more, then she quietly tip toed up the stairs to her bedroom to recollect everything that had transpired that evening from the beginning to end. She was happy to have met this boy named Joe, glad her brother had invited them to go to the movie, and glad they had enjoyed time sitting in the swing together. This was the best summer of her life and she wanted to keep it going. She noted of her happiness with Joe in her diary.

The next morning before noon, her sisters and some friends gathered on the front porch of their house planning a trip out to the creek for a play day in the water and sun. Now the creek was not deep enough to actually swim in, but at least one could lay along-side the water in the sun and then get wet to cool off. It was a quiet place in the edge of the timber where they would not be bothered by any people. Actually there really wasn't a beach, but at least there was some sand to sit on. Joe showed up with the other guys to join them for the trip. Now, to get to the creek they had to walk about three miles and then three miles to get back home. There were a few dangers associated with this adventure such as snake bite, a confrontation with a coyote or wild dog, or even an injury of some sort. Their mother knew what they were doing and where they were going, and not being one to worry, she only warned them to just be careful. She had a positive attitude, and trusted God to watch over all of them. No one seemed to mind the distance they had to walk, as they were happy being together, enjoying this day and each other. Yvonne had quickly eaten a bowl of cereal before she rushed out the door to join the group. Also, no one was in the habit of taking much food or water with them on these trips. So with very little planning for the day ahead, the group started out on their swim adventure.

As they walked north to the edge of town, Mrs. Gray waved and hollered to them, "You kids be careful and have a nice time."

"Hi, Mrs. Gray, thank you," several of them chorused as they skipped on down the road. The walk to the creek didn't seem to be long at all, with all the chatter amongst them. Every step was an adventure to living. The last three hundred feet became a race to see who could hit the water first. It was beginning to become quite a warm day. The cool, clear water was soothing to their bodies, especially their feet. Everyone splashed and kicked, getting as wet as possible in the shallow water. That was the trouble with the creek, being so shallow. Still, it was the only way for them to enjoy some fun since they had no transportation to a pool or lake. The boys wrestled in the water, while the girls splashed and pushed any time they got a chance. Joe joined in the play with everyone. Laughing, splashing, and basking in the sun, enjoying every moment.

After hours of play, Elaine spoke, "Remember when Mark brought a watermelon for us to share last year? We lay in the water eating it and spitting seeds at each other."

"That was great," shouted Johnnie as he jumped in the creek again. "I wish we had one right now, I am getting hungry. Maybe it is time to go."

"You know, I am getting hungry," whined Yvonne.

"Me too," quipped Rich. "My breakfast is all used up."

Everyone agreed to leave. They had been gone from home for about four hours. Walking about one mile, Yvonne began to feel quite weak, dizzy, and even nauseous. The long afternoon had warmed up, and they had spent much energy playing in the water. She thought some lunch or snack would be great. "I'm sorry guys, I don't know why I feel so bad," Yvonne whimpered. "I think I really need something to eat." She tried to keep on walking, but thought she might fall down, so she sat down alongside the road in some shade.

Joe looked worried." What should we do?" he asked as he put his arm around her.

Rich said, "I can hurry on up to our house and see if we have any kind of snack for you to eat."

"Really, Rich, that would be great," replied Yvonne. "I am going to sit in the shade here and wait for you to come back."

Joe sat beside Yvonne. "Hurry guys, I will stay with Yvonne." Rich and Johnnie were already walking as fast as they could to their house. Yvonne put her head on her knees. She was worried as to why she felt so bad, for this had not happened to her before. Yvonne's sisters joined her and Joe in the shade to wait for the guys to return. It seemed to be a long time until they saw the boys coming around the curve. Yvonne felt more nauseous, hungry, and worried that she just might pass out. Joe tried to comfort her by rubbing her back and he kept asking, "What can I do?"

Yvonne teasingly whined, "Do you have a candy bar in your pocket?"

It wasn't too much time, they could see the boys approaching. As they got closer, Yvonne thought she could see a loaf of bread in Rich's hands. "I'm sorry but this is the only thing we could find," he cried as they reached them. "We searched the kitchen and this is the best we could do."

Yvonne thought that a loaf of bread never looked more appetizing. "It looks wonderful, Rich." After eating one piece, she immediately began to feel better.

"Thanks guys, this is just fine. I love bread." She really did feel better, eating another piece. Everyone else had a slice too. After eating a third piece, she stood up, taking a deep breath, said, "Okay, I feel better, we can continue on our way." Everyone was looking at her as they rose beginning the walk on to home. Frankie started laughing commenting how wonderful a piece of bread could taste.

As they passed Rich's house, Yvonne said, "Rich, tell your mother thanks for the bread, I think it saved my life." Everyone cheered, but she sincerely believed it did save her day. At least, it saved her from feeling any worse than how she felt a few moments ago. What else could they have done? They could not call her mother or anyone else to come get them. This loaf of bread seemed to have been a good solution. They continued walking until finally everyone was home at last. Joe walked past his uncle's house, wanting to make sure that Yvonne made it all the way to her house.

Yvonne said," See you later, Joe, I need to eat something more and take a shower."

"Me too," replied Joe. "See you later. I'm glad that you are okay." Off he went down the street.

Later that evening, Joe stopped by with his mother as they were on their way to his home once again. If Joe was not working for a farmer, his mother insisted that he return home so that he would not be a burden to her sister. She worried that Joe might be a problem, she did not want that. "Mom is taking me home again. Sorry, I have to go. I had fun today, see you soon."

"It's all right, Joe, I understand. Bye."

Her diary pages were way too small to write everything she experienced, but she jotted down as much as the page would allow.

Joe surprised Yvonne arriving at her house with a friend, who had a car, on Saturday afternoon. She had not expected to see him this soon. Joe hollered out the opened window of the car as it rolled to a stop. "Hi. I asked my friend to drive out here so I could see you. I thought maybe your sister could go with us sort of on a double date?" He was smiling from ear to ear.

Yvonne starred at him for a moment before she could speak. She turned to her sister and whispered lowly, "What do you think. Do you want to go?"

"No, I don't think so, but you go have fun." She whispered back. So Yvonne got into the car with Joe and his friend, although she was uneasy about it since she didn't know Joe's friend. They drove away as Joe questioned her, "Why wouldn't Doris come?"

"I don't know, Joe, she just said no."

As they started down the road, he said, "I thought we could get something to eat and go to the park. After stopping for drinks, Joe commented to Yvonne that Harry is disappointed and wants to go back home as he is not enjoying being a chauffeur for us." Joe was not happy as to how the situation had resulted. This was the best plan he could conjure up to be with Yvonne. It didn't work out the way he imagined, so within a very short time, Harry drove back to Yvonne's house, dropping her off. Joe kissed her, reluctantly got back into the car, and the two boys left heading back to the city.

The night was still early as she entered the house. Her sisters and some other friends were gathering things together for a pajama party. So she joined them, which it is never too late to join a pajama party. These all night parties transpired quite frequently during the summer. All the girls wore their pajamas, talked all night, laughed about everything, played tricks on each other, ate any snack they could find, and tried to be the last one to fall asleep. It was always a very fun time causing everyone to be totally exhausted the next day. The girls (because it was girls only at a pajama party) asked Yvonne about Joe, his friend, and what did they do?

"We just drove around for a while, got a soda at the Root Beer Stand, talked about going to a movie, but Joe's friend decided he would rather go back home as to hang out with Joe and I. So they brought me home and that was all." The conversation continued on about a movie that Doris had seen, and so into the night the girls partied.

The weekends usually brought cousins to Grandma's house. There was a lot going on at Grandma's house every time the cousins arrived. Grandma and Grandpa had nine children, who each had at least two, five, or seven children. That's a lot of cousins. All of the children, except one lived less than fifty miles away from Grandma so it was not a big deal for them to show up at Grandpa and Grandma's place, which everyone called home. Hanging out with the cousins, could be fun, or not, it just depended on each situation and the mood some might be in. They sometimes played soft ball or kick ball, or sometimes argued about what to play or how to play, but whatever happened, they were glad to be together. Love really did exist among them in spite of their foolish actions and arguments. Grandma had a potluck dinner at her house, for which Grandpa made some awesome tasting barbeque meat on his grill, while Grandma and her daughters mixed up potato salad, corn on the cob, fresh bread, green beans, and fresh baked blackberry cobbler. Oh yes, homemade ice cream to top off the cobbler. Delicious! Each of the children would take a turn at cranking the manual ice cream maker until only Uncle Mason was the only one still able to turn the crank and the ice cream would be frozen. Yvonne enjoyed every gathering at her grandma's. Good times were always enjoyed.

Chapter VI

Yvonne was happy this summer, she could hardly believe her good fortune. Vacation Bible was completed, so ending her first attempt at teaching. She had fun working with the children, singing happy tunes, making crafts, trying to keep them in control. Her birthday had turned out to be wonderful, since it included meeting Joe. She had her first date, first kiss, and first experience meeting a boyfriend's parents. She was happier than last year for sure. June of 1961 was almost finished.

July 4th was the next holiday to celebrate, for which her grandma usually hosted a picnic at the lake or at her home. Cousins, aunts, uncles, many relatives shared food, much play time, swimming, and fireworks. July 4th was just one of many family times with grandparents and cousins. Always each summer there were week-end camping trips with aunts, uncles, and cousins. These trips were also active with swimming, surviving the sun, water, heat, and insects. Some trips consisted of maybe ten people, or possibly twenty-five. One never knew which relative might arrive to join.

The 1961 4th of July celebration was to be different from previous years. First, mother prepared a family dinner, after which the family was going to the city park for the concert and fireworks. Joe begged his mother to bring him out early that day so he could join Yvonne's family dinner and the concert. Yvonne would play in the Municipal Bank, and it would be his first time to watch her play. His mother brought him out to the wishes of Joe and Yvonne. They were delighted to be together this 4th of July.

Dinner with the family was pleasant and delicious. Everyone was pleasant and in a good mood. Yvonne helped to clean up dishes, excused herself to change clothes. All members of the band wore white. She wore a white blouse, white pleated skirt and white sandals. She considered herself to be neat, simple, and attractive. Of course, everyone would look the same.

Yvonne joined the rest of the band in the outside stage at the park. All the parents, families, friends, and others in the audience sat in lawn chairs or on blankets on the grass. The band tuned their instruments, before beginning to play the first piece. Once during the concert, Yvonne peeked out into the audience to see Joe. His smile caused her to blush, so she quickly looked back at the music to pay more attention to what she needed to do. Of course, she did not want to mess up tonight. The music was patriotic with mostly marching tunes, which were her favorites. The audience applauded as they were pleased with the performance.

After the concert, Yvonne spread a blanket on the beach close to the edge of the water to watch the fireworks under the stars! She was filled with so much joy to be with her new friend, she thought her heart would almost burst. This 17th summer of her life had taken such a pleasant turn, she hardly knew what to expect next. Tonight she thanked God that she had met Joe, that the concert went well, as the fireworks burst with fantastic colors! She and Joe sat ever so close, commenting on the colors and shapes and sound of each firework as it exploded overhead. Yvonne glanced behind her to get a glimpse of her parents. It seemed that they too enjoyed the evening and were much in love.

Joe's affection for Yvonne grew every day. It took a lot of effort on his part to stay away from Yvonne for any length of time. As far as he was concerned, his desire was to be with her every day. He did spent some time with the boys around town so as not to give Yvonne's parents cause to complain. He was not too sure if they approved of him. Yvonne told Joe that her parents accepted him, otherwise he wouldn't be allowed in the house.

In the times away from Joe, Yvonne did other activities. One day she rode to the stock yards with her uncle Henry. He was her youngest uncle of whom she was very fond, and he lived next door so they were close as far as residential arrangements. This provided her easy access to his horses for riding. She went to pick blackberries with her sisters and mother. This was not such a fun activity as they walked possibly six to ten miles on a hot day, getting scratched from the briars, possibly sunburned, and the next day covered with chiggers! Oh what hardships to endure for the sweet taste of blackberry pie or jam!

Sunday, as were many Sundays in the summer, Yvonne went with her uncle Henry, who also owned a ski boat, on an outing to the lake. At least, one of her uncles or aunts would usually ask her to go with them, for they knew she enjoyed being out on the water, but she was also a good baby-sitter for their children so their parents could also enjoy the activities. On occasion, they would even allow her to drive their boat. She was very thankful to have such a close family with which to be a part of. She did not mind watching the little ones in exchange for a day on the water. These fun times filled her youthful days. Yvonne had been boating with either one of her uncles, or her brother since she was about eleven or twelve. She had learned to water ski at this young age and every summer, looked forward to these adventures with her relatives.

Yvonne thought a lot about Joe wherever she was boating, babysitting, or at home. It was difficult for her to not see Joe when he was at his house, she wondered what he might be doing. Telephone calls were possible, but Yvonne was not allowed to make long distance calls. That was an expense her parents did not allow except for special occasions. Joe would occasionally call Yvonne, but he too was limited to the length of time of the call. Since Joe could not drive without a driver's license, and neither of them had a car to drive, they just had to survive without seeing each other as often as they would like. She would worry that perhaps he had forgotten about her when she didn't hear from him, but then he would call and she would be fine again once she heard his voice. They both knew they had to make the best of the short summer because when it ended, the future was unknown.

Joe managed to come to town again, in time for another annual event, which was the cemetery picnic. This was an evening event for people in the surrounding area to work together in order to raise funds for the care of the cemetery. A chicken dinner was served, music was played, bingo, and other games were available for all. All the profits went to the care of the cemetery. Children were free to roam the cemetery and the adjacent field. Almost everyone knew everyone who would be there. It was a big challenge for the youngsters to take a walk in the cemetery after dark. Yvonne and Joe had a wonderful night just walking around the grounds, holding hands, and being with each other. When it was time to go home, Joe rode with her family to their house. Again, they went to sit in the swing to end the evening quietly together.

They thoroughly enjoyed being together, wishing their time together could go on indefinitely. Of course, some of her sisters or friends were always near, so they were never actually alone very much. Yvonne's parents liked that aspect of her so called dating. They did not have to worry about her, and never wanted to see her in trouble or hurt. Yvonne always had mixed emotions each time Joe had to go home with his mother. She was never sure when he might return or if he might forget about her while away. She never needed to worry, though, because Joe never wanted to go to the city ever. He wished his family lived closer so he could see Yvonne anytime he desired. They went swimming, when possible, walked around town most evenings, and many nights were spent on the porch with others, or in the swing out in the yard. All good times got recorded in her diary.

Yvonne's parents surprised her by making the final payment on her high school class ring, and presented it to her. She could wear it with pride. Her brother had gotten a class ring in high school, and Yvonne wanted one very much. She had paid as much as she could come up with, over the past six months and was trying to save enough to pay it off. Now her parents graciously made the final payment. It was a lovely ring, the most expensive piece of jewelry or anything that she had ever owned. With the gift of this ring, her parents expected her to finish high school in return for them helping to pay for it. Oh yes, she wanted to finish high school. Yvonne liked school a lot. It was the one thing she knew for sure. She felt so much pride in finally having the ring to wear, and would gladly finish school.

"Thank you, Mom and Dad for getting it for me." She hugged them both and kissed them on the cheek.

Chapter VII

Each spring, Mr. Burch planted a very large garden in which the entire family helped with planting, pulling weeds, or harvesting. In the spring potatoes, plants, and other seeds were buried in the black soil. By the end of summer, whenever the potatoes were large enough, they had to be dug up and stored for the winter. Digging would be all day duty for the whole family, getting dirty, picking up all the potatoes, and hauling them up close to the house. Mr. Burch plowed open the rows so the potatoes became exposed to the surface, and the children picked them up, putting them in a bucket and then carried them up into the yard. Barefoot was the way to do it because the earth was, soft, cool, and felt good. Otherwise, your shoes would fill with dirt quite fast and would make for uncomfortable walking. Sometimes a potato barely poked through the dirt and had to be dug out by hand. Mom came behind everyone to make sure all the potatoes got retrieved. It wasn't such a bad activity. Actually, it could be fun to see how many potatoes there were, and see who might find the largest one. The family depended on this garden and especially the potatoes to help provide food for the winter besides what was purchased at the store. After everyone passed over the dug up ground, it would again be plowed through, always finding more potatoes the second time around. As the potatoes got carried up to the yard, they still had to be sorted into two piles, one pile consisted of potatoes that had gotten cut, broken, or had a bad spot. The other pile was made of the good ones. The potatoes would lay out in the yard for a day to dry off. Digging potatoes was a huge job, but everyone felt good for being a part of the winter's food supply.

Saturday was often a bigger day as it was Mr. Burch's birthday celebration. He always planned a fun party for his own birthday, figuring if you had to get older, you might as well enjoy it.

Mom had to do a lot of cooking for family, relatives, and friends. Guest arrived about noon, bringing lots of delicious food. It was indeed a grand time with food, fun, laughter, and love. Adults played card games, talked, drank beer, while the children ran around the yard chasing each other. The party represented thanks for the garden crops and happiness for family and friends. Everyone had a hell of a good time. The party would last all afternoon into the night. Dad and everyone else became totally wiped out after a day of hard work and a day of fun. Sometimes, Yvonne wondered whether her dad's party needed to be so big or crazy, but she conceded that he worked hard all year, so why shouldn't he celebrate?

By Monday, we all were in need of rest, but that was not always the way it transpired. The potatoes had to be transported again into the basement, into a large wooden bin. The yard had to be raked and cleaned of debris, and garden tools had to be put away. No one complained too much about these choirs because they knew it was standard procedure.

After these events passed, everyone knew that summer was more than half over. There seemed to be a little more urgency to getting things accomplished before school started. Yvonne had been working diligently on a sewing project, which was to be a surprise for Joe. The next time he arrived at her house, she presented him with a shirt which she had sewn. Actually, she had made matching shirts for Joe and herself.

She handed Joe the package to open. He had no idea what it could be. His face lit up with a huge smile, as he held the shirt up to gaze at it with much amazement. "Wow, you actually made this for me?"

She smiled as she replied, "I did."

"This is wonderful, I can't believe that you could or would do this." He gave her a big hug and said, "I can hardly wait to wear it. When shall we wear them?"

"We can wear them anytime you would like to." She answered still smiling at his pleasure.

Joe tried the shirt on, smiling as he walked around the room with much pride. "Thanks, Yvonne, I love it, and so glad you made us shirts alike."

"You are very welcome," she said as he hugged her right there.

Later that afternoon, they were able to collect a few bicycles for a ride out to the swim hole, where the two of them walked around holding hands, sitting in the shade, and reminiscing about the fun days this summer. All the activities Joe experienced with Yvonne were new ones to him. These good memories were inventoried and stored in both their minds. That evening, after finishing dinner, again they walked up and down the streets of town until late sunset. Walking was their main past time together, sharing funny stories, or just being together in the silence. This was a big part of their happiness. There were very few times they watched television (only if it was raining). After walking, time was spent sitting on the porch alone, or with family or friends. Sometimes talk was serious, but mostly a joke was told, or a funny situation was retold. Every fun filled day of the summer was going by much too fast. No one could slow it down. No one could add a day to it. Time had to be dealt with regardless of where, when, or what was happening.

Yvonne knew she was going to return to school to finish her last year. Joe wasn't certain as to what he was going to do. He had no desire to go back to his school in the city. He might consider going if he could go to the same school where Yvonne attended. That was not possible as his parents lived in the city too far away. He could not live with his uncle in the country full time. He had to make other considerations about his future. Joe told her of the heated discussions he had recently with his parents. They were pressuring him to make a decision of which he had two choices; one he could go back to school, or two, he could join a branch of the service. His dad wanted Joe to enlist in a branch of the service. His mother preferred he finish school, but if not, then she agreed with the service. Joe said he wanted no part of either one. So against his own wishes, Joe had to obey his parent's decision to enlist in the Navy. He explained all this to her speaking slowly as if the words just didn't want to come out. His face had the saddest expression she had ever seen.

He knew he didn't want to leave Yvonne as he was happy with their new friendship. Joe knew in his heart that he would miss her more than anything, even though their friendship had begun only three months ago. In his mind, he truly thought he was in love with her, and the only way to keep her for his very own was to marry her. He thought that marriage would secure their friendship, their love, their future, and the wonderful feeling he had when he was with her. This thought reigned high on the list in his mind. Joe didn't have a clue how marriage would work for them, just that it might connect them forever. He mentioned his plan of getting married to her, which surprised her because they were so young.

Yvonne was sad to think of him leaving. She knew without a doubt that she would miss him. Each of her two older brothers had enlisted in the service and left home. She knew how she missed each of them when they were gone. However, Joe and his parents thought that this was an opportunity for Joe to engage in something that would teach him skills and provide him a way to earn a living in his future. This plan would take the burden off his parents, giving him a chance to take responsibility for himself and his future. He could learn something new and be paid for his time.

Once this decision had been made, Joe brought up the subject of marriage to Yvonne every time they talked. Yvonne never understood why or how he thought they could be married at this time of their lives. They were so young! How could marriage make their lives better, or solve his problems? Marriage, as Yvonne understood it, presented many more problems for them, such as; where they would live, what financial means would provide them living expenses, and what if she became pregnant? There were far too many unanswered questions for her to undertake such a huge step. As much as she liked to be with him, she thought neither of them was mature enough to proceed with this plan of marriage. Never less, talk of marriage came up so often that Yvonne just let him ramble on rather than try to put an end to his conversations. He asked her every day, sometimes more than once. She thought marriage was his fantasy so she allowed him the opportunity to talk about his dream. When he insisted on an answered, her reply was; that she had to finish school first. "My father only gave me permission to date when I turned seventeen. Do you think he would even consider marriage?" was her final statement to his constant asking.

Joe usually tried to come up with some solutions such as; "You can still finish school while I am gone." That was true. She just could not picture herself being married, going to school with her friends, and still living at home with her parents. Again Yvonne reiterated the fact that her parents would not approve, and since a written consent from their parents would be needed, she knew it would not happen. With an unplanned pregnancy, quitting school would be necessary. That was not going to happen!

"Joe, we are only seventeen, this would not be a good thing. I need to finish school, after that I will consider a marriage proposal. But not at this time."

"Yvonne, I love you, will you marry me?" Joe would plead.

"Joe, I love you too, but I will not marry you right now," was her reply. He would get a sad face and sort of hang his head, but he knew she was right about this important part of their lives.

September arrived soon. Joe's family made plans to spend the week-end on the river with some of their relatives. He invited Yvonne to come along. She packed a couple pair of shorts, a swim suit, tooth brush, and went with Joe and his family. The drive to Red Bud was a very nice trip, as now she had become more comfortable with his family. Still her excitement increased as they traveled, for she had camped many times with her family, however, she had never been camping with anyone else, nor had she been to this particular place on the river. This time would be a very different experience with strangers, except for Joe. Joe had become everything to her since their first meeting at the beginning of summer. She would be all right as long as he was beside her. As the miles rolled on, Joe chatted with Yvonne telling about his cousins that she would meet.

"Robin and Sherry are cousins who are our age." He stated, they will be good to you. "Also my cousin, Jerry, Aunt Becky and Uncle Clem, and Aunt Sarah and Uncle John will be there." He continued. She tried hard to remember each name. She kept telling herself that this trip would be compatible to others with her own family, so she tried to relax and prepare to meet all the new people. Nervously chewing on her fingernails, she listened to Joe ramble on.

Arriving at the cabin, Joe proudly introduced her, "This is my friend, Yvonne."

"Hi, Yvonne, we are happy to meet you," Aunt Becky spoke first, others chimed in with hello. Yvonne replied, "Hi" several times. They gradually approached the cabin in which they all would be staying. Her relatives always did the tent or sleep in the car type of camping. How strange it felt to be with these people instead of her relatives on this Labor Day week-end, which was usually the last camping, swimming excursion for the summer. Everything was going swell even though she was terribly nervous.

Joe beamed with happiness having Yvonne with him. All the relatives were surprised to see that Joe had a steady girl, but were most friendly and did a great job of making Yvonne feel welcome.

Joe's cousins talked catching up on news, while Yvonne listened intently. She was learning more about Joe as each one told stories about him, trying to embarrass him and possibly Yvonne also. Jerry said, "Remember last year when Joe fell off the boat before Uncle Clem got it docked." Everyone burst out laughing. It was all in good fun. This small group was progressing in getting to know Yvonne as well as having a good time.

Robin added, "What are you going to do for us this year, Joe?"

Everyone laughed and looked at Joe as he replied, "Wait and see."

The adults prepared the evening meal, while the young adults helped serve, and clean up afterward. The food, social time, and the beautiful evening, made for a beautiful summer night in southern Illinois. The group of teens continued their conversation and fun, hanging near the river and staying out doors after sunset. Soon Robin brought out a board game and called out, "Would anyone like to play?" So they settled down to a game of monopoly. Popcorn and other snacks were provided. Yvonne was pleased how the day had evolved as she always had seen events happen this way on the television, but not so much in her life. The laughter, the game, the snacks all continued for hours. Jerry claimed the victory at the end.

Joe and Yvonne went outside for a short walk under the moon and stars. Joe wrapped his arm around her waist as they strolled along the river. No one wanted the evening to end, especially Joe and Yvonne. There was tomorrow to look forward to so everyone began to find a place to call their sleeping spot. The girls took one room and the boys another. They said, "Goodnight," with a sweet, "see you tomorrow," to the boys, as they separated. But the girls were up for a while getting to know each better like girls usually do. Finally, they tired from the long day and all succumbed to sleep.

The next morning arrived much too soon for all the party kids. After consuming some awesome pancakes, Joe and Yvonne went for a boat ride down the river with Uncle Clem. Joe had asked him to take them for a ride after the men returned from fishing. Yvonne had ridden in a boat many times, but never before had she done so sitting next to a boy whom she liked so much. The sun felt warm, not too hot. The view was different because of being on the river, versus a lake. She had enjoyed the fun with other teens, the conversation with new friends, the food, and being with Joe. She struggled to accept that all of it was real. Returning from the boat ride, the other teens met them on the bank. Yvonne took pictures of the girls and Joe's sisters.

After dinner, Joe's family packed their bags to return home. Everyone said their good-byes. Robin said, "Yvonne,

I hope you come back next year. It was fun getting to know you."

"Thanks, Robin," she replied as she entered the car. All the way home, Yvonne played the events of the week-end in her mind over and over. She had thoroughly enjoyed every minute of it. She would never forget this Labor Day weekend with Joe's family and how happy she had felt just being with Joe. Joe, too, was happy as a lark after the awesome time with Yvonne and even with his own relatives. He didn't chatter quite as much on the way home, but relaxed sitting next to Yvonne enjoying the feel of her body next to his.

"Arriving at Joe's house, everyone quickly grabbed bags out of the car and settled in for the night. Yvonne thought it had been a good trip for everyone. Sometimes things could go wrong, but she had not noticed any problems. Preparations for Joe's birthday would begin tomorrow as he too would now be seventeen. The two of them would be the same age, not that it made any difference before, but Yvonne loved the idea that they both would be seventeen!"

Early in the morning, Mrs. Small went shopping for groceries and then Yvonne helped Joe to put them away. His mother baked a cake and prepared a special dinner for Joe. Joe and Yvonne helped his mother when they could, but mostly they sat in the swing on the porch and went for a walk.

It was a bitter-sweet birthday, with Joe trying to enjoy every minute of it. Yvonne wanted Joe to be happy, yet they both knew this was their last day together for a while. Yvonne was going back home tonight and Joe would be leaving for the Navy. It was difficult for them to not think about tomorrow and just enjoy the moment. They did their best.

Joe's mother drove them to Yvonne's house once again, this time dropping off Yvonne for possibly the last time until who knew when. Joe kissed her several times not wanting to leave her. Each time it was to be the last kiss, but another would land on her lips. The hardest part of the day had finally arrived, saying, "Good bye for now." Yvonne's mother never said good bye, she always said, "See you." That was the way Yvonne wanted to leave it. Finally, with tears, they broke apart. Joe reluctantly entered the car and she watched him leave with his mother. He waved to her for as long as he could still see her.

She kept watching as the car turned the corner, and stood there, motionless except for all the huge tears running down her cheeks. What had happened this summer? This was the most exciting, fun summer Yvonne had ever experienced. She couldn't believe it was ending. She tried to capture every moment of it from the day she turned seventeen. It was all so much like a dream that she had to reassure herself that all of it actually happened. She really had no idea when she would see Joe again. She promised to write him often. Joe said that he would count on her letters to sustain him while he was away. She knew in her heart and her mind that he truly was depending on her to help get him through this time of being apart.

Later that night, Yvonne told her sisters all about the wonderful week-end, the new friends she had made, and the fun they all shared at the cabin. "I met Robin, Sherry, and Jerry, who are Joe's cousins, and his aunts and uncles. We played monopoly, walked along the river, and went for a boat ride." She said, "We actually stayed in a cabin with rooms and beds."

After exhausting all details, she retreated to her room, gathering paper and pen, and began writing her first letter to Joe.

Dear Joe,

I cannot believe that you are going to be away for such a long time. I miss you already just thinking about it. I think we had a fabulous summer, the best ever for me, I hope you enjoyed it too. I liked your cousins, for we seemed to be quite a bit alike. Hopefully, next summer we can spend another weekend with them and the rest of your family too.

I think I love you, but with this being my first experience with a boy, I'm not sure just what I feel. They say emotions range from puppy love, infatuation, a first love, and real love. I know you think we have real love. I hope it is. I know that you are my first love and I hope it will last forever. I hope that you will understand why I said that we could not get married. I think you honestly know that it would not be possible as we would need parent consent. We can wait until I finish school and then make plans. I do love you.

Again I say that this summer was so much fun as I cannot stop thinking about it for one minute. I will never forget the things we got to do together for the first time. I will remember the walks, talks, movies, swimming, camping trips, hanging out with everyone, and just the two of us being together. I hope that this summer was enjoyable for you too. (I think it was.) Being with you added so much more to each day of my life, and makes me thankful that we met. I want to tell the world how wonderful you are.

I always look forward to going back to school, even though I hate to see summer come to an end, but since you will not be around, I will carry a little sadness within me. I can hardly wait to tell my friends about our summer.

I hope that you like where you will be and that the daily routine will not be too hard. My brothers have told me about military life, so I have a bit of an idea of what you have to deal with. Try to enjoy whatever moments that you can and learn as much as possible. I think it is exciting to think about all the places that you may go and all the new things you might get to see as you travel. I am most envious of that part of your journey.

I love you and miss you already. It is time for me to go to bed. Be good. I will write again tomorrow.

Love,
Yvonne

Finishing her letter, she reread each word and thought about adding more, but knew there would be more letters to write in days to come, so decided to let it be. Thoughts of Joe swam in her mind as she pondered how her life would continue with Joe so far away?

The summer of 1961 was over. It had been the most fun, most exciting, summer for her. Her mixed emotions of summer ending, and school beginning were always conflicting, this year more than any other was special, as she had fallen in love. Her friendship with Joe was as free and happy as any two young people could wish for. Yvonne wasn't a hundred per cent sure what love consisted of, but knew what she felt for Joe was genuine and whole. What would take place in the future, she knew not. Would she fall from her cloud of happiness, or would her life develop into a happy fairytale?

Chapter VIII

Yvonne tried to sleep in allowing the children time of watching cartoons by themselves. Regardless of how tired she was, thoughts of Joe's accident kept flooding her mind. She desperately wanted some answers, the sooner the better, so maybe she could understand what had taken place that last awful night of Joe's life. Realizing she was getting nowhere with her thoughts, it was time to face the long day. Descending the stairs to join her babies in the kitchen, cereal was the choice of all. The kids liked cereal the best because they could help themselves without their mom having to prepare it.

She put on a little smile saying, "Good morning."

"Mom," Dolly started, "what do we do today?"

Yvonne joined them at the table pouring cereal in a bowl. They each ate quietly waiting for their mother to instruct them for what lay ahead for today, this night, and the near future. "Today I need your help." She began as they all looked at her. They could sense her despair, sadness, and the nervous way she spoke. "We need to select clothes for us to wear tonight and tomorrow. Then I need you all to be very good at the funeral home tonight. There will be lots of people at the visitation coming to see Joe for the last time."

"Mommy, will Tess and Joey be there?" Dolly asked.

"Yes, they will."

"Good, I want to see Tess again. She must be very sad."

"I know she is very sad. Tess loves her daddy very much." Yvonne choked. "Lots of people will be sad and that is okay. Let's remember our manners and please be good." Yvonne thought of other things to say, but didn't want to overwhelm them with too many instructions. She knew her mother would be present to keep watch over them. Of course there would be other children in attendance, so her's would not be alone. They could visit together in the room downstairs.

Jesse spoke, "Can we go outside to play today?"

"Yes, you may, then after lunch we all need to get our baths and get dressed. So until then, you can play outside or whatever you would like to do." Yvonne felt that she needed as much time to herself as possible to prepare for the afternoon hours and into the night. She knew she must reserve her strength for what would transpire at the funeral home. Trying to keep calm and tearless was about all she could handle right now. They all finished their cereal, excused themselves, and dashed off to their bedroom to get dressed.

A few phone calls helped the morning pass. People were very kind with their condolences and generosity of food which some had brought to the house. A few neighbors dropped by to offer sympathy and food for her family to enjoy. Sympathy cards arrived in the mail. Yvonne was amazed at the number of people who had heard about Joe and were extending their kindness to her. The lady across the street came over to visit. The information she had collected was that Joe had been at the bar for most of the afternoon and evening. He had a lot to drink. Yvonne was shocked at this bit of information. *Why had Joe done that? Why had he not called her?* It was straining her nerves and emotions hearing this news. Yes, she knew that he could do some drinking, but why that day? If only he had called her. The other bit of information which she received was from the police report stating that he had swerved off the road crashing into a compacted pile of dirt. The crash caused him to hit the back of his head on the glove box knob therefore causing him to bleed to death very quickly. In fact, he was probably unconscious on impact. That was terrible to visualize, but she needed this info. All these facts were very disturbing for her. *"Why" was the word that kept surfacing in her mind over and over.*

The day after Joe left for the Navy, Yvonne attended her first day of school as a senior. She felt happy, excited, yet sad as she rode the bus for the ten miles. Her thoughts ranged from all that had transpired this past summer to wondering what Joe might be doing. Everyone boarding the bus was joyful, happy, and noisy as they hollered their greetings. There were a few more grade school students than high school. That was cool, for Yvonne knew each one, and one in particular always liked to sit with her.

The ending of each summer was always a bummer, but getting to see friends at school would be refreshing. She couldn't wait to tell her girlfriends, whom she hadn't seen all summer, about Joe. This news about her new friend this summer was hardly believable to her, let alone getting her friends to believe it. She could imagine how amazed they would be, since they had known Yvonne for years, and she had not had a boyfriend before.

Entering the school building, Yvonne saw Kathy, "HI, how are you?"

"Great, how about you?" she smiled as they walked down the hall. "What is your first class?"

"English, of course."

"Me too, see you there."

She also saw Sandy, Betty, and Barbara plus some others. They didn't have much time to talk right then for they had to get to their first class.

Throughout the day, Yvonne found herself thinking about Joe, wondering where he was and how he was coping with his new experience. Finally at lunch, she got a chance to tell Kathy and Sandy about Joe. "I met someone this summer," she began.

"Yes!" they both answered in surprise.

Yvonne shook her head. "Yes, his name is Joe. We had a fun summer, swimming, movies, and dates." She spilled the information quickly. "He had to sign up in the Navy now, but we are writing each other."

Kathy asked, "How did you meet?"

"He stayed with his uncle in town to do some work for farmers. He worked with my cousin and others guys, so my cousin, Frankie introduced us. He is cute. We had fun."

"Yvonne, this is exciting. I can hardly believe it," Sandy exclaimed. The bell rang. "Oh great, time for next class," she retorted. They all started off down the hall. "See you later."

Yvonne knew her friends would have a surprised reaction. It made her smile seeing their faces. She was anxious to tell Betty also. In between classes and after school, she got to spread the news to a few more friends. Yep, just as she thought, surprise on their faces.

The first day of school was over quickly as it always was. She didn't have enough time with her friends. Tomorrow she would tell them more about Joe. It was great being back in school as Yvonne thought it would. She was happy to be able to finish her last year in school. She was happy to have a class ring to wear, and happy thinking about Joe.

It was the next week before she received her first letter from Joe. She was getting anxious about not hearing from him, although she knew he would be very busy in boot training and really would not have time to write. As she walked into the house, she saw the envelope on the buffet. Picking it up, she hurried out to the swing into the yard, where she opened the letter to read.

My dear sweet Yvonne,

Oh how I do miss you. I feel like I am so far away from everyone, I can hardly stand it. Thanks for your letters. I have received three so far. I love you too, very much.

I have met some neat guys from all over the states. There are a couple of guys my age. It has been very hard getting up so early every morning. How I wish we could go to the creek swimming. I miss you.

I think I will try to come home at first chance. If I complete all my training satisfactory, I might be able to get a short leave. I sure do miss you. Please write to me again soon. It is so hard being here without you. Sorry this is so short, but I have so much stuff to do I can hardly find time to sit down. I miss you and love you.

Love always,
Joe

Yvonne was absolutely thrilled with Joe's letter even though she thought it was very short and without much information. However, she read it again before slipping it back into the envelope. She went to her room where she tucked it away in a dresser drawer. Later that night, she reread it then wrote him her response. Her letters seemed repetitive also, in that she kept talking about how wonderful summer was, how much she missed him, and how it was good to be back in school. She hoped her letters would not be boring, but that was all she could think to write. She did tell him how her friends were surprised that she had a boyfriend! She told him about each class and about her promotion in band. This was her life now, what else could she write about. She tried to be regular with writing the letters, trying to get one in the mail each day or at least every other day.

Some days Yvonne received two letters and then there were several days when she never received any. Although his letters were short, Joe soon brought up marriage in his letters. He always said he loved her and thought they should get married. How many times would he say that? She wished he would just leave out the marriage stuff. Yes, she liked him a lot, but was not ready for marriage.

Each day school activities increasingly filled her time. The normal classes occupied much of the day, playing in the band called for extra practice each night, and the girls' athletic group met one evening a week after school. Still she never for a moment forgot about Joe. Her thoughts of him were on her mind all day. Sometimes, she daydreamed of the past summer activities with Joe. On most Friday nights, the band marched at the home football game. Marching was a high light of her music participation. Marching in parades and presentations at football games were a challenge, but fun to do. Participating in the band had given her a reason to attend many of the sports activities.

She still did some babysitting whenever a relative or neighbor would ask. This was a way to earn a few dollars. Roller skating was the usual Saturday night activity during the school term as the rink was closed during much of the summer, and the rest of her time was involved with girlfriends, but mostly just with her sisters. A school bus from another small village, of Sorenson, stopped at their house, picked up anyone who wanted a ride to go skating. All the parents appreciated this bus service since the children were able to enjoy an activity and their parents did not have to transport them. The school bus would be filled with laughing, singing kids. Yvonne never missed a chance to go skating, becoming quite skilled. Occasionally, her friend's mother took the two of them on a week night. Yvonne appreciated all offers the other parents gave her to go skating, to a movie, or other school event. They were supper nice to include Yvonne. Yvonne's father did not appreciate getting out of an evening to go anywhere since he got up so early each morning.

One day, a large envelope came in the mail addressed to Yvonne. She had no idea what it might contain. Upon opening it, she found an 8 X 10 picture of Joe in his uniform. Oh my, was he ever attractive! Wow, Yvonne was so proud of her guy. Her eyes could hardly believe how handsome he looked. Now, she definitely had something to show the girls at school.

"So this is Joe?" was Kathy's response.

"Yes, it sure is," Yvonne replied.

"Let me have a better look," Sandy requested. "Where did you meet him?"

"Like I said, he stayed with his aunt and uncle this summer down the street from where I live."

Barb said, "I like his smile."

"Me too, Barb," Yvonne replied. "Got to go, here comes the bus. See you tomorrow."

The next night as she was studying, the telephone rang. Yvonne answered, not having a clue as to who it might be. "Hello."

"Hello, sweetheart," came the voice through the line. Yvonne could not believe her ears that it was Joe. Her face lit up bright as a spotlight. "Hi, I can't believe that you are calling," she replied, almost a shriek.

"We each have a couple of minutes to call home, so I chose to call you. I miss you so much I can hardly stand it. Your letters sound as if you are having so much fun in school that you probably don't even miss me."

Yvonne, was shocked to hear him say that, then replied, "Oh, that is not so. I certainly do miss you. I am only trying to enjoy my last year of school."

Then Joe continued with much excitement, "I will be home for a visit in November. I can hardly wait."

"Really?" Yvonne blurted, she could not believe that he could come home so soon.

"I know, it doesn't seem real to me either, but I am ready to see you." He replied excitedly.

"That's great. Do you know what day it will be?" she asked. Then she heard someone yelling at Joe that his time on the phone was up.

"Alright sweety, I guess I have to give up the phone for now. Write to me soon. You know how I love you."

"Bye, Joe, I'm glad I got to talk to you." Hanging up the phone, she stood still in shock. First, she received pictures, and now a phone call. Wow, she was floating on cloud nine. After finishing her homework, and writing a letter to Joe, she went to bed, but sleep would not come, for she kept thinking about Joe, how their relationship was developing, and wondering how will she feel when she sees him next in his uniform?

Two months passed, but not fast enough for Joe as he was deeply homesick. He missed his bedroom, family, mother, but mostly, he missed Yvonne. She was the number one thought on his mind all the time. He got to know some of the guys in his group, telling them all about his girl, how they had met, how much he loved her, and that he would someday marry her. A few of them understood his joy, while some just nodded their heads in agreement. Joe developed his plan concerning Yvonne and the next time he would be seeing her. He was anxious and happy to carry out his surprise on the visit home.

October passed quickly, with football games coming to an end and then November continued to fill the days with school work, band practice, roller skating, and baby-sitting. The boys basketball games started, which meant that the band would be playing at half time. This senior year of school for Yvonne was progressing swiftly.

Joe always liked to surprise Yvonne, so he never told her the date of his arrival. One day, there he was at her front door. Her heart jumped as she viewed Joe in his white Navy uniform, she could hardly move her legs to make contact. Extending her arms she hugged him with all the strength and love she could muster. At this moment, after more than six weeks, she realized how much she actually did love him and how badly she had missed him. Her affection for this person had grown since their meeting back in June. Now she realized what it was to care about someone so much. Neither of them knew what to say. They kept hugging and smiling.

Joe had his surprise planned out and could hardly wait to put it in motion. He pulled a small box out of his pocket.

Yvonne had a look of surprise as she thought, what is this?

Holding the small box out to her, he said, "Open it." His heart pounded with happiness. Happy to be with Yvonne again, and happy to give her this surprise which he thought would seal his love for her.

As she opened it, he pleaded, "Please say you will marry me, Yvonne."

She was shocked by this unexpected gift, not that he had brought a gift, but for what kind of a gift. She stood there with her eyes wide and mouth open. Yvonne stared at the ring box as her hands were shaking. It wasn't very long ago that she had gotten her class ring, which she knew how much it had cost, so she surmised that this ring also was costly. She looked at Joe with puppy eyes trying to show him her love, yet wanting to be cautious as to what she was about to say, "Joe, I told you before that I want to finish school."

"I know, I know. Just say you will," again he pleaded with that awesome smile. He kissed her.

All the times before that Joe had talked of marriage or all the times he had asked her to marry him, she always thought he was kind of playing with her, not being really serious. Starring at the beautiful ring, she was afraid to say anything more. This was serious business. She thought she loved him, but this was the first time in her young life in which she had come to a decision this important. She thought, am I grown up enough to be engaged or get married?

Joe was so excited to give Yvonne the diamond ring, he could hardly contain his happiness. He made a decision to buy a ring, planned how he would make the down payment, and then pay the remaining amount in six monthly payments. This was a super big day for him. Now, looking at her staring at the ring, he didn't know what to think, because he just expected her to be so happy and say, "Yes." But she did not. He would not give up on her, for he loved her more than he could express. Finally he said, "Let's go out to eat and to a movie. We can talk about it."

"Sure," she replied. "Give me time to change clothes." Yvonne didn't know what to do with the ring. She thought she could not wear it because everyone would ask questions. She put it in her dresser drawer for a safe place to keep it.

All during the meal, Joe talked about getting married. "Yvonne, aren't you going to wear the ring I got for you?"

"Joe, I'm afraid what my parents will say."

She tried to steer conversation away by asking him questions about the Navy, "Tell me about what you have been doing, who are your new friends, and where will you go next?"

"I don't want to talk about that." He replied. His answers to her questions were short, and then he went right back to the same marriage topic. Yvonne was apprehensive to accept the ring. She felt very special that he wanted her to be his wife. She understood the commitment Joe had taken on to purchase the set of rings. She was pleased that he loved her. She just could not wear the ring with the intention of marriage. School was foremost in her plans, besides, she knew her parents would not approve.

They managed to enjoy the evening, movie and the special time together. Joe was a bit upset that she did not wear this beautiful ring, upset that his plan did not quite work. She tried to keep smiling the whole night, although she knew he was disappointed with her decision.

Joe went to the high school basketball game with Yvonne on the next evening. This presented an opportunity for her friends to see that Joe was for real, really cute. Yvonne was not trying to keep her romance with Joe a secret, but she didn't want people thinking that she was getting married soon. Their love for each other and the smile on their faces shone for everyone to see. She was proud sitting next to Joe, at her school, among her friends.

The next day was an enjoyable time together as she stayed with Joe at his parents' house. On Sunday, he had to return to his post in Virginia. Joe's uncle was driving him to the airport and Joe asked Yvonne to ride with them. Of course she wanted to go, giving her a chance to be with him a little while longer. She was extremely quiet all the way to the airport, thinking of how much Joe had become a wonderful part of her life, and yet she could not make the marriage commitment. Joe held her hand and whispered sweet words to her all the way to the airport. She understood more and more how much Joe cared for her. She loved his attention, affection, and being with him. It was very difficult to say good bye once again. Joe held her hands, looked her in the eyes, and asked, "Please say you will marry me and wear the ring. Please."

"Joe, I love you, but I just can't say yes right now." So with a very heavy heart and sad look on his face, Joe finally had to walk away to board the plane. Yvonne stood motionless as a statue until Joe disappeared, then she entered the car with her head hanging down and tears on her face. As Joe's uncle drove away from the airport, Yvonne looked out the rear window of the car until the airport was no longer in sight. Tears rolled down her cheeks most of the way home. Never had love been so prevalent in her life. Never had anyone shown her so much attention and respect and care. Her heart ached with happiness and sorrow pulling her thoughts to and fro. She very confused on the marriage issue. Joe's aunt was comforting to her as she reiterated such an experience in her life. It was a solemn and sad ride all the way home. Yvonne hardly knew these people with whom she was riding, and yet they were the ones to comfort her and be patient the whole time.

Upon arriving home, she thanked them for the ride, entered the house and quietly prepared for bed and school the next day. She didn't want to talk to anyone, just wanted to be alone with her thoughts. *What was happening with her life? She was happy to have met Joe, yet time was moving too swiftly for her. She did not wish to live in the fast lane as they say. What would she do with the ring? What would her parents think about marriage? She knew they would not approve, but would they actually allow her to proceed with it? She was not ready to move away from her family, knowing she was too dependent on their support and security. She took the ring out of the box to carefully look It over once again, then replaced it back in the box in the drawer. The ring was beautiful! Still, she could not imagine wearing it. She wrote in her diary of her love for Joe, her happiness, and her unsure emotions.*

In the morning, she climbed out of bed, got dressed for school. She viewed the ring with a longing in her heart, then quickly closed the box and closed the drawer in which it lay.

Meeting with her friends at school, she received many good comments about Joe, and well wishes of happiness for her. Yvonne was pleased that her friends approved of Joe, but she just couldn't tell them about the ring. What would they say? She was still confused about the whole marriage thing. It would be a big commitment for her to wear the ring as a promise to marry Joe, and somehow, she felt that commitment would put a shadow on her activities at school. She didn't feel very good about having the ring under those circumstances. She knew her response to the ring was a disappointment to Joe, but she just didn't know any better way to handle the situation, and she was not ready to give Joe up by breaking off their relationship. The ring remained a secret tucked away in the dresser drawer. Yvonne didn't tell her sisters, Frankie, or anyone about receiving the ring from Joe.

The exchange of letters continued, only now Joe called on the phone more often and wrote a little less. He was anxious about her lack of commitment and disappointed that she would not wear the ring, or at least say that she would marry him. Yvonne was sorry that he was so worried and upset, but she knew her commitment about finishing school was stronger than any plans to get married. Her parents never said a word about what she was doing concerning Joe, but she knew they were in favor of her finishing high school. They never scolded, pushed, or made much comment to her in any way, shape, or form.

In her next letter to Joe, she tried again to explain her hesitation about marriage. He would not like her reasons, which she understood. *What else could she say or do? To her, this was the most sensible plan for her life. This was the decision she made, however confused she remained.*

My dearest love,

What a surprise you gave to me! The ring is absolutely beautiful and I imagine expensive. I am so sorry that I cannot at this time commit to wearing it. I have told you many times how I need to finish school. My parents insist. I am afraid they would not agree to any marriage and probably frown on an engagement. I am sorry to hurt your feelings this way. When you surprised me with this situation, I had to make quick decisions. I am not good at that. I've thought about it over and over. I do love you, but I just have to wait for marriage.

All my friends at school think you are quite handsome. Me too! I am glad you went to the game with me. I enjoyed all the time we had together. Too bad it couldn't have been longer.

Please understand that I do love you. This is such an exciting time in our lives. We must embrace our friendship, love, time together. Life is short. You know that, right? That's why you want to get married. I get that. Just know I do love you.

Love you, love you
Yvonne

Chapter IX

Classes at school came with challenges, requiring more study time. She had to write reports for English class and journalism. She practiced her instrument a lot on her own and with the group to compete at the local and state levels. Each day proved troublesome for her to concentrate on homework, because she was engrossed with thoughts of Joe. The end of the first semester finally arrived. The Christmas holidays were almost upon them. Besides the usual family celebrations, Joe would be home for a second visit. The thought of him coming home again brought excitement and anxiety to Yvonne.

She was apprehensive of Joe's visit this time because of his comments of her activities at school and in general while he was away. He implied that she should maybe stay home a bit more and not be having so much fun. Yvonne could not understand why Joe made comments such as those. She knew he had a strict schedule to follow, but his situation should not determine what she could or could not do. He had to deal with his daily duties the same as she did. The fact that he could not be near her was not Yvonne's fault. She would sympathize with him on the loneliness he was experiencing, trying to understand his situation, but was not convinced that she should change her pattern of activities. She never dated anyone else, never attempted to, or planned any such thing which would hurt Joe. She stayed true to him in every way, never crossing the line to be with anyone else.

Regardless of the complaints which Joe had written in his letters or said on the phone, his arrival home once again was exciting, happy, and exuded warmth for this girl who was his world. Yvonne again welcomed him with open arms. She was a bit mystified as to the comments he wrote her and yet his open happiness toward her exemplified otherwise. Their love for each other had grown stronger with the passing of time. All complaints seemed to have been forgotten. The time apart seemed long but very short as once again they were in each other's embrace.

Being together for their first Christmas was the greatest present in itself for each of them. On Christmas day, they celebrated with dinner and time with her family. Yvonne gave Joe an 8 X 10 picture of herself, which was her senior picture. He gave her 'Chanel No 5' perfume. She had never had perfume before, but what she had read In a magazine, Chanel was expensive. It pleased her that Joe figured it to be something appropriate for her. Having Joe with her this holiday was the best gift she could have hoped for. That evening, they traveled to Joe's family home to spend a few days, which turned out to be more relaxed than the first visit back in the summer. They both admired their parents for the hard work and dedication they had exemplified in raising each of them.

The day after Christmas, Joe and Yvonne enjoyed a night at a movie. They were much more at ease with each other settling down in the theatre. While they watched the movie inside, it was snowing outside. This new snow brought smiles to their faces. Snowflakes are made with such intricate patterns which give each flake a beauty all its own with a design fit for a queen. Yvonne could sit for long periods of time viewing this miracle that God presented the world. Exiting the building, they stood in the snow as she lifted her face upward to allow the lovely, cool flakes land softly on her face. Joe took her hand asking, "Want to go for a walk?"

"Yes, yes I would." She replied. They left with no destination, no planned route, just the two of them holding hands. The streets, sidewalks, and trees were lightly covered with the beautiful white flakes. The snow sparkled under the street lights. The stars twinkled clearly in the sky. The night was incredible in that its perfection surrounded them with peace, beauty, and love. The moon shone its light on them as the snow softly fell slowly around them and on them ever so light and fluffy that the flakes landed with but a whisper. Walking in silence, they were in heaven wrapped in the serenity that only God could have placed upon them. This night, this walk, and this snow seemed to have been all put together just for them, a night never experienced before or ever again. Yvonne did not want to stop walking with the man she loved in this dusting of snow under a moon that glowed with a quiet stillness that presented them the earth as if it were theirs only. She wished their walk would continue on forever. She wished they could walk until they would be carried away into their very own happy-ever-after land. It was a perfect night, they were a perfect couple, and the world was a perfect place.

Each day that Joe was home, they enjoyed every minute of their time together, going to the movie, playing board games, walking in the snow, but there was still the problem of Joe's unanswered question. Actually, Yvonne had answered, but not with the answer which Joe would accept. Finally, on his last day of the visit, Joe made the statement that he did not want to say, "Yvonne, if you will not promise to marry me, and if you are not going to wear the ring, then I need to return it."

What? Oh no! Hearing these words upset Yvonne very much. Of course she understood, but it finally hurt her to realize that it had to be one way or another. She cried. She ran upstairs to her bedroom.

He followed, begging her, "Please keep the ring, please wear it, and just say that you will marry me."

She was crying as hard as she ever had blurting out, "No, I can't," with huge tears rolling down her cheeks. Then Joe took another step toward her, reached for the ring, and as he stared at her with the saddest eyes in the world, he hugged her as he kissed her forehead, then slowly turned and walked away. She felt very close to this person she was getting to know, but reality kept holding her back. She wanted to run after him exclaiming that she would wear the ring and marry him after she finished school. Instead she stood frozen, shaking, as she watched him descend the stairs and walk out the door.

Joe called her several times from his home yet that night to say bye, and asked again, "Yvonne, are you sure you won't wear the ring?"

With a crack in her voice, she replied, "I'm sorry, Joe." She broke into tears wondering as to whether she was doing the best thing for her or for Joe.

He said, "I love you," for the one hundredth time, hung up the phone and was gone once again. This was a very disturbing, difficult day for her.

The correspondence between them continued with more passion and many emotional words than before. He still loved her, but yet, did not understand her refusal to accept the ring which he wanted so much for her to wear. Every letter from Joe was filled with pleas of marriage, if she would not marry right away, at least would she please make a commitment for the future. He had gone through much effort to purchase a ring for her. All he wanted was for her to wear it.

Yvonne worried for days about whether she had made the right decision, yet she was not convinced that the two of them were ready for a life of living together. In her mind and her heart, she knew their parents would not permit marriage. Their letters continued to flow back and forth across the waters as he traveled the ocean, and she continued with her senior year of school.

The next semester brought more homework, new classes, and new challenges. In February, Joe sent her two valentines! He did so because he loved holidays and surprises. She was pleased and again considered her future with Joe. He was very expressive and romantic as his notes and cards expressed. Honey, I love you more than anything. You are everything to me. "Please be mine. I love you."

Along with the thoughtful words, were other words of agitation mentioned in his letters stemming from the denial of marriage. Written in every letter to Joe, was always her explanation of why they could not get married. Maybe if she said yes to marriage in six months or a year, he would be pacified? She thought what he wanted was just more than she could promise. Finally, Yvonne made even a bigger decision. With a heavy heart, many tears, and a lot of doubt, she wrote a letter of which she never imagined that she would ever write, especially to Joe.

Dear Joe,

I am sorry to write to you this letter. I find it difficult to continue our relationship as it is. I care about you and enjoy writing to you as often as I can. Your letters, however imply that I am not faithful to you and carry false accusations of which you have no confirmation. You have been a wonderful addition to my life for over six months now, and maybe it is too soon to end it. I am trying to finish my high school education as best as I can. Of course, I want to have fun but I am not dating anyone and there is no one else that I want to be with. I just need to enjoy each day with friends and participate in the activities at school. It is my last year. There is no reason that I should feel guilty over these activities just because you think otherwise.

I am sorry that you are so far away and lonely. I wish you could enjoy what you are doing for now, realizing that it won't be so very long until we could be together again. I don't want to keep getting letters from you which cause me to feel bad about my activities in my life here at home.

We had a wonderful summer and many good times since we met. I can't believe it has come to this. I am confused and unsure of how to handle our situation. We need to grow. Three summer months is very little time together to know each other very well. It is with regret on my behalf that I our relationship has come to this. I wish you the very best of luck in your career. I thank you for loving me, for all the fun times we had together, and for respecting me. Good-bye.

With love,
Yvonne

She wrote and rewrote the letter several times, trying to get each work correct, not wishing to hurt his feelings, but to release her of the bond they had and the intent of marriage. She cried a lot as she wrote each word, thinking about what this letter would produce for them. She waited a couple of days before mailing the letter, trying to be sure of what she was doing. Yvonne had totally enjoyed Joe's friendship which had gone on for less than a year. She thought she had really loved him, but now she was thinking she needed to let it go, to experience more of life, to perhaps get to know a few other people, perhaps finding the same love or even something better with someone else. She really didn't know what she expected in the future, she just had to find out what might be there, other than with Joe. They wrote each other several more times, questioning the breakup and reason for it. Joe promised to be more patient toward her, but the loneliness would play games in his mind. Yvonne thought of reconsidering her decision, but worried about how that would rectify anything going forward. Their correspondence gradually became fewer, then ceased.

Her diary filled with unhappy thoughts.

Joe was always anxious for mail call. Any day that he received a letter from Yvonne boosted his moral twofold. If per chance he did not get a letter on a given day, he would read the previous one again or even several of the past letters. Her letters were his only contact since he was so far away out in the ocean. Excitedly, he opened this new letter which he could tell was her hand writing. After reading the first sentence, Joe could not believe the words he saw in print. He slowly finished the whole page in disbelief. He folded it up then headed up to the top deck of the ship with the letter, and his favorite picture of them in his hand. Standing on the open deck in the moonlight, he read her letter again and yet again. Tears rolled down his face. *Why is she doing this? I thought she loved me as I love her. She is everything to* me. *I need her, I love her, I will not let her go.*

Joe stayed there with his thoughts and grief late into the night. He was on a ship in the middle of the ocean with the moon and stars. He felt his whole world shutting down with silence, darkness, and loneliness surrounding him. He stood for hours staring at the moon, stars, and water, wondering how he could have lost the first person whom he had truly loved. There was no one to live for, to love, to hold close to his heart. How could he survive without her?

The time for Yvonne to leave the house arrived all too quickly. She dressed, helped the children with their clothing and then, with everyone seated in the car, she drove into town to the funeral home. It was very difficult walking into the funeral parlor as she was shaking terribly. She had not a clue how her life had come to this-a funeral for her husband. Thank goodness her parents, siblings, and Joe's family were all present, waiting for her arrival. She needed to be strong to get through this night, and with her family around to support her, she hopefully would be able to.

After receiving hugs from loved ones, she gradually approached the casket, knowing what she was going to see, having had the vision in her head all day. It was as she had pictured, even better. He lay there as handsome as ever: too real, too still. The man whom she had loved since the day they had met. *Why, Joe? Why did you leave? I did not want you to ever leave me.* All these pleadings kept going through her mind. All the memories she had of the two of them together trickled through her thoughts, even back to their very first meeting. If she wasn't thinking of their past, then she was wondering why he had to go.

Tears streamed down her cheeks, as she wished to go back to 1961, when they were so young, so happy. She wanted to live her life over from the beginning with Joe, the way he always wanted it to be. Truth be known, she wanted to scream, yell, and fall on her face to express her pain and loss, but that would not be proper, here in public, in front of everyone. She kept her composure as best she could for the present time. When she arrived home once again, she knew she would fall apart crying to God to help her through each day without Joe.

Every person, family member, friends, and co-workers lined up to greet Yvonne, to wrap their arms around her, and express their sympathy and sorrow. They all shed tears as they viewed Joe so still amongst the flowers. Exchange of conversation was comforting to her as all spoke words of kindness. The evening seemed an eternity for Yvonne to keep standing, but she would not leave Joe's side all night. Joe's mother was greatly upset to see her son so motionless, knowing she would not see or talk to him again. He always caused her to smile, for he loved her much.

Both of his parents were torn with broken hearts. Yvonne's friends and Joe's friends hugged her, encouraging her to look ahead as there would be better days. *How could there be anything better than what she and Joe had?* She had only been with Joe for about two years this round, and now he was no more.

The children were very good throughout the evening, not causing any disturbance as the family pulled together, helping Yvonne get through this ordeal. The number of visitors who were present, expressed to Yvonne and the Small family how well liked Joe had been. She just kept thinking how short their time had been together. After the twelve year separation, finally they had gotten married, and now he was gone so soon. Yvonne's life had been quite a roller coaster since her high school days. Why had it been so? Her life pattern in her dream, was to get married, have a family, and be happy. What happened?

Climbing into bed at last, Yvonne was absolutely drained. She felt nothing. There was no desire to dream, plan, think, or cry, although many things and questions kept creeping into her mind. *Did she dare to dream of Joe and all the good and bad times together? Could she possibly plan for the next day or week or year?* She tried to keep her mind on all the comments that people had made at the visitation, which had been pleasing for her to hear. *What was it George said about Joe's insurance? Who was the last person to talk to Joe?* When her mind became boggled again with all the conversation, all she could do was cry. How many days would she cry? *Why? Why did this happen?*

Yvonne did not sleep very well, but the world did not stop turning either. Morning did arrive with the sun in the sky as it was the day Yvonne had kissed Joe for the last time. She wanted to rewind the clock, take the calendar back. She did not want to fulfill her duty for this day. She had to be at the funeral with the children before noon, set through the service, and then go back home without Joe, for the rest of her life. She prayed that God would be her strength throughout the day and days to come. She finally mustered up enough courage to begin this day, descending the steps to move on.

The children were sad to see their mother in such a state of despair again. They wished she could be playful and even commanding as they knew she could be. They had their breakfast and got dressed as she requested. She was pleased with her little ones' behavior through this difficult time.

Arriving once again at the funeral home, the children walked in with their mother, found a seat with their grandparents, and watched their mother walk up to the front. Yvonne approached the casket one last time, whispering to Joe, "I love you always, from the beginning and until eternity." She stood there trying to retain in her memory every last detail of his physical features. Finally, she took her seat in the front row, fearing her knees would buckle before she reached the chair. This was her last goodbye to Joe, she felt very empty and alone. *Was this how it was for Joe on the ship so many years ago when he had read her letter of goodbye? Oh, the pain and sorrow one felt and how much more sorrow could one come to suffer?*

Yvonne was so engrossed in her sadness, she didn't notice right away the empty seat next to her. The entire family was seated behind her, so why one empty seat? Then she saw her favorite uncle Henry appear and sit down, taking her hand in his. She was so relieved to have someone beside her, especially her uncle who would love and support her. She knew that he would understand her situation the most since he had recently lost his wife to cancer. The two of them sat there, just holding hands and taking comfort from each other.

Yvonne wondered how long she would be able to keep Joe's scent, his touch, his smile, his love in her memory? She hoped it would never fade. She could hardly concentrate on anything that was being said, all she wanted was to be in Joe's arms. Uncle Henry squeezed her hand several times to let her know he was there. She tried not to cry too much, although tears continued running down her cheeks. There really were not words that could ease her pain at this time.

As the service ended, people hugged her and wished her better days, each offering help with children or anything she needed. It was quite a long ride to the cemetery in the limousine with the children. The sun filled the blue sky creating a pleasant atmosphere as they rode. The children chatted quietly about the long, awesome limo. It cheered her to hear their comments about the luxurious automobile. Actually, it was Yvonne's first ride in a limo, so she appreciated their excitement. The funeral concluded with a final prayer at the gravesite.

Once again everyone hugged her and wished her well. They said their goodbyes with good wishes and promises to see each other soon. Gradually, everyone drifted away, leaving immediate family to transport Yvonne and the children home. She didn't want to be alone, but at home is where she would feel the closeness of Joe. Now, she had to begin the rest of her life, this time, without Joe, forever.

Part II

Chapter X

Besides normal school activities, Yvonne began making plans for the senior trip. She had dreamed of this trip since beginning high school. She intended to go even though some of her close friends were not planning to go. Sandy, Kathy, and Barb would be going. Betty, Linda, and Sue decided not to go. This would be the last chance to be with some of the other students before the school year ended. She thought this trip would be a good experience for her traveling with classmates rather than family. Her goal of this trip was to gather memories for her to cherish the rest of her life. Tales of her brother's senior trip encouraged her to participate in her own class trip.

There was one huge problem to tackle for this endeavor. Her wardrobe was in sad need of some new clothes to wear each day of the trip to Chicago. Her plan to improve this situation was to use the babysitting money which she had acquired over the last few months, to buy enough material to make three outfits and save a little to spend during the trip. She purchased enough material, cut the patterns, and did the sewing each evening. In this busy time, she still had thoughts of Joe.

Maybe she should not have written that last, "Goodbye" letter. Maybe she should write him once more to see if he would accept her back. Perhaps, she had destroyed the best chance for love in her life and would not get another. Nevertheless, she had done what she had done and now must live with the outcome.

Spring Prom was another big event taking place at school. Juniors and seniors planned, prepared, and decorated the gym. Boys asked a girl to attend the fancy party. Yvonne dreamed all through high school about this glamorous party, but figured she would not be a part of it. First, a boy was not likely to ask her, and second, she could not afford a formal dress to wear. Yvonne was sure this dream would not become reality. In fact, she did not get asked to attend the event, however, a decision was made that the jazz band would play when the regular band had intermission. Yvonne was a main player in the jazz band, so she would be going to the prom for this reason, but not with a date.

It was not required for her to dress up, just wear school clothes. There was no need to come at the beginning, only in time to set up the music. The jazz band would play from the band room which was at the end of the gym, upstairs. There was an opening in the wall so the people in the gym could hear, and the band could see into the gym. It was somewhat of an honor for the jazz band to play at the prom and for her to participate. The performance went very well, playing for approximately a half hour. The students applauded and cheered, which pleased the members of the band.

After putting instruments and music away, most of the students left the room quickly, some returning to the prom dance. Yvonne did not leave the room right away. She stood at the opening of the gym for a while just gazing at the decorations, the girls in their formals, and the guys in nice suits. The gymnasium looked very nice as it represented a ballroom. Yvonne was happy for all who were able to attend and for them to enjoy the night. She was sad that she was not more of a part of this popular event for her last year of school. She sighed, realizing her father would be waiting for her in the parking lot. She hurried down the steps hoping no one at the dance would notice her leaving.

Arriving at home, she joined her sisters in their bedroom to tell them all about the prom, how it was decorated, all the pretty dresses she saw, and how she wished she could have actually been more a part of it all. "Everyone seemed to be having a fun time," she said as she turned to go into her own room.

Doris spoke, "I'm sorry you did not get to dance."

The senior trip scheduled for the end of May, arrived. Students and chaperones began boarding either one of the two large chartered buses, with a destination for Chicago. Yvonne was filled with anticipation. She did not get to participate in all the events during high school, but this was a big one and she was definitely a part of it. All her efforts were paying off. Most of her clothing was new and all freshly packed in the suitcase which she had also purchased at the thrift store.

The ride on one of the two deluxe excursion buses, with about thirty of her class mates on each bus, reminded her of the one day school trips she had gone on in grade school. The guys and girls chatted and sang and laughed every mile of the way. Everyone's adrenalin was pumped to the max on the five hour ride. There was not a lack of entertainment on the whole trip. John stood in the aisle to perform a solo of his favorite southern song. Everyone cheered and clapped. Yvonne smiled as she watched and listened to all the chitchat, singing along with the songs she knew, and enjoying the company of all.

Arrival in downtown Chicago was late in the afternoon. Yvonne could not take her eyes away from the view out the bus window. There were so many tall buildings, lots of traffic, and people going everywhere, much more than what she had seen in St. Louis. Each student eagerly waited in line to find their luggage and proceed to the entrance of the large hotel. This was definitely a new adventure for her as she had only stayed in a small motel a couple of times with her family. The numerous floors and rooms in this awesome hotel, with elevators to run the people up and down, was completely overwhelming.

Together with her roommate, Sharon, they found their designated room and examined it with much pleasure. Sharon didn't seem too happy to be rooming with Yvonne. Yvonne did not have much interaction with Sharon during the school years, but thought she could manage rooming with her for a couple of nights. The teachers had paired the students as to who would share rooms, so she and Sharon would have to manage for a couple of days. After exploring their own room, comparing with others, expressing their pleasure of the large hotel, everyone dressed in nice attire to gather for the evening meal.

Dinner was served in a glamorous ball room with crystal and silverware and everything elegant. There were many uniform dressed servers to bring the food and drink. Yvonne thought she was completely underdressed, even though she wore her best. She used good manners and tried not to spill her drink. She followed others' example so she might not do something foolish. For her, this appeared as a scene out of a movie—the room, the food, and the servants!

Halfway through the meal, her nerves finally began to relax a bit so that she could enjoy the food and time with her fellow class-mates. She listened to all that transpired and enjoyed the meal as it progressed through all five courses! As everyone finished the meal, students began to leave the large dining area, eager to be on to the next adventure. Some lingered in the lobby, while others returned to their individual rooms. But not many succumbed to sleep very early even though it had been a long day already. What transpired through the night, Yvonne did not know for she stayed in her room. She had not a clue what others might be up to and felt safe staying in.

The next day, the class enjoyed several tours around the big city. On one excursion, a boat cruised along the shoreline of the lake. This reminded her of the trips she took with Grandma, aunts, cousins, mother, and sisters on the U.S.S. Admiral on the Mississippi River. Those were fun cruises with family. This was different as one sat on a seat with open sides where the view of Chicago's many tall buildings were prominent from the water. It was a slightly windy day, but nice and warm. Yvonne took pictures of her friends and the landscape. She wouldn't remember the names of all the buildings, but had captured the overall scenery in pictures of her classmates, the boat, and the big city.

After lunch and the tours had ended, there was free time before the evening meal. A group of six girls thought it would be an adventure to ride the monorail through down town Chicago. Kathy and Sandy thought they had it figured out how to travel in one direction to a certain point, exit one tram, jump on a returning tram which would bring them back to the hotel. The plan worked well until no one could remember what street to exit on.

For fear of getting too lost, they decided to get off at the very next exit, rather than ride too far the wrong way. Because of this mistake, they had to walk several blocks to the hotel. Being in a big city was scary and exciting at the same time. Everyone agreed that next time they would consult with an adult or take one with them. Still, they laughed about their tour as they rode the elevator to their rooms.

A musical was on the schedule after the dinner meal. The production happened to be a new popular one which anyone should be thrilled to see. This musical was performed in a huge, beautiful theatre. It would be Yvonne's first time to watch live actors perform on stage. She watched the action with much appreciation for the actors speech and singing abilities. Some students didn't care for this type of a show, but Yvonne enjoyed the new experience. At the end of the musical, the classmates returned to the hotel, where some were up late into the night once again trying to find extra entertainment any way they thought to be fun, such as dropping water balloons to the street from the tenth floor! Yvonne joined in and even dropped a few balloons herself! She felt excited to be part of such behavior, but slightly anxious that they might get into trouble. It was just fun!

This class trip proved to be as good as she had hoped. The money she previously earned was spent justifying a dream. She was pleased with the effort she had invested and believed her brother Daryl's information and encouragement for the trip had proven to be worthwhile. The memories from each day was now stored for future reference to be enjoyed always.

The weekend came to an end all too soon. The students boarded the chartered buses for the trip home. On this return voyage, there was less noise and commotion. Almost everyone was quite worn out from three days of activities and getting a little less sleep than normal. Yvonne relaxed in her seat, reviewing the past few days, as she drifted into a light sleep. All the excitement which she had built up inside her for the four years was now gone, but never to be forgotten.

The graduation commencement was on Friday of the next week. This was the ceremony for which she had worked so hard. It had been her parent's dream that all their children reach this goal of graduating from high school. She was pleased to have accomplished this for herself and for her parents. She felt excitement, but also sadness, as graduation presented an end of an era for her. No longer would she see her friends on a daily basis. No longer would there be bus rides to school, homework, band practice, football games, and sharing of good times. She had earned her diploma, reached her goal, only to be at a lost as to what she would do next. When Daryl had graduated, he wanted to continue his education going to college, but there were no funds to pay for it. She knew it was the same situation for her. Maybe, possibly she could find a way to go through nurses' training? Not even that seemed to be possible. What would she do?

Yvonne became upset before the ceremony, when she learned her father was driving the family to the school, but would not attend the graduation. How embarrassing! Most of the other kids drove themselves or at least had their parents in attendance. Her father had just dropped them off at the door. Part of her achieving this goal was for her parents. Now it hurt that her father would not be present to actually see her presented with a diploma.

Most likely, other students didn't realize that her father was not at the commencement, but she did. Yvonne held her emotions intact through all the speeches, awards, and announcements. When the diploma had been given to each student, Yvonne realized that this was totally the end (the end of school that is, the end of her life as she knew it). Everyone began cheering and clapping, excitedly hugging and congratulating each other. Tears slipped down her cheeks. She was slightly embarrassed and quickly wiped them away.

A few students noticed and laughed of her foolishness. "This is a very good day to be happy," someone chirped.

Yvonne knew that was true, but still felt loss of something important in her life. This part of sharing, growing, and learning was over, now everyone could move on to something new. Yvonne wished she could be as happy about her future, but school was everything to her, the most important activity in her life. She was not ready to give up on learning, being with friends, or any of the school activities. Her parents always encouraged her to do the best she could, stay in school, and be educated so she could do what? All of a sudden, the end of school was here and Yvonne had not a clue what would be on her path henceforth.

Chapter XI

School ended, graduation was over, now a new summer 1962 had arrived. This beginning of summer definitely didn't seem the same as previous ones for Yvonne. She didn't possess the usual excitement for freedom and fun to be enjoyed in the sun, for she knew that this summer had to go in different directions than previously, now that she had graduated. A full time real job was her plan to start earning some money so she could at least buy a car and start taking on more responsibilities for herself.

She applied at a few different places where she thought she might be able to work. Of course, she didn't have experience for any type of vocation, whether a secretary, waitress, or factory position. Also, she didn't know how she would travel to the job, but would figure that out when the time came. A few weeks passed without being able to acquire employment. She tried to enjoy the warm weather while waiting, but knew the usual summer fun wasn't in the program.

Thankfully, one of Yvonne's friends, Trish, figured out a place for Yvonne to work. Trish's father operated a mobile home lot where they sold house trailers. Trish convinced her father that Yvonne could work for him answering the phone and whatever else he would have for her to do at the trailer court. So Yvonne acquired her first job working at a mobile home sales lot.

This business was only a mile from her home, therefore making it accessible for her to travel to her new job via walking, bicycle, or catching a ride with someone going that direction. Mostly, she rode the bicycle. Her main task was to answer the phone whenever it rang, take notes on messages, and relay them to her boss. Occasionally, when a used trailer was traded in, she cleaned the inside. A great amount of time was quite boring, for she was alone in the office waiting for the phone to ring most of the day. Trish would often call just to chat. Yvonne didn't mind being alone, and was grateful that someone would pay her to basically sit and wait for the phone to ring.

One day after work, a salesman brought a '55 Chevy to their house so she could see it and her father could check it out also. Edward had found this car which he thought Yvonne might be able to purchase. She fell in love with it the minute it stopped in front of the house. It was a shiny black and white two-door sedan with nice black and white interior. Even though the car was seven years old, Yvonne could not find fault anywhere! Her father inspected the motor and mechanics and agreed to cosign a note for her to become the owner of this Chevrolet. Yvonne could hardly believe it, a car of her very own, how sweet! Dad made sure she understood that she was to pay for it, not him. "You know that you have to make the payments on this car and provide your own gas."

"Yes, Dad, I will do that. Thank you for helping me." She gave him a great big hug. She knew she would pay every penny of it because this car was a dream come true. Now she could go to town whenever she chose, or roller skating, or where ever she decided to go. Most of all, she had transportation to her place of work!

Working at the trailer lot all summer, prohibited going swimming with her sisters whenever they were going, nor could she participate in the all night slumber parties if they took place during the week, nor could she sleep until noon if she was tired. She was okay with not doing all these things that she did in her past, because paying for her own car was important. Of course, Yvonne still got to go boating with her uncle on the weekend and a few other summer activities like playing in the Municipal Band.

For sure, this summer was totally different than past ones. Yvonne spent more time helping her mother with laundry, ironing, preparing meals, washing dishes, and anything there was to do around the house. She had helped in past years, but now had a better appreciation of the amount of work her mother did each day to keep the family moving. It was a valuable learning session for doing laundry, cooking, etc., preparing her for being able to eventually live on her own. Each year, as she aged, she realized the extent of hard work her mother did daily.

Getting up in the mornings to be at work on time was not a chore, as her father had been a good role model when it came to holding onto a job. He never missed work as far as she could remember. He worked day after day, week after week, even overtime whenever he could to bring home a good pay check. This job was part of a goal so she could purchase her car. There was no way she would quit working, for any reason.

Thoughts of Joe were on her mind most days, especially at work when she had nothing in particular to occupy her mind. In the evening when her sister's friends gathered on the porch, Yvonne would sometimes join them, bringing back many good memories of last summer. *Where could Joe be at this time, and what was he doing? Why couldn't she have met Joe this summer instead of last? Would she ever hear from him again?*

Yvonne still wanted to keep the memories of last summer in her mind forever, for they were good times and pleasant ones. These thoughts were precious to her even though she wasn't adding more to them. *But what if Joe would contact her? Would that be great? Could they have another fun summer? Would he still love her as before? He had at least another two years to serve in the navy. Maybe he has moved on too.* Neither her cousin, nor any friends in town heard from Joe or mentioned him anymore.

Yvonne wished she had the courage to talk to Joe's uncle to find out where he might be and what he may be doing. She never did ask his uncle, or try to contact any of his family, or even try to write Joe another letter, thinking that probably his address was different by now since guys in the Navy got transferred around a lot. She also thought Joe might not want to see her again.

June and July passed even though work was somewhat boring. Yvonne hoped someday she could find a better position, especially one more interesting and paid more. Sundays involved church and family gatherings. Many of the boating, swimming, and camping activities were much the same as in the past. Again she would tag along with either her brother or one of her relatives who owned a boat.

The family picnics, skiing and boating, some camping, and a slumber party or two on the week-ends were still activities she could do. Her parents did not take a vacation trip this year, so she would not be missing out on an adventure with them.

This summer of 1962 was quite uneventful, unlike the summer before, when she had met Joe and had so much fun. The more she thought about Joe and the fun last summer, the more she missed him. Reflecting on last summer, she wondered if she had made good choices. *Why had her life transpired the way it had? What would come next? Will she meet Joe again or someone else?*

It was a good thing when the roller skating rink reopened, presenting Yvonne a chance to join the fun. It was also the best thing to do on Saturday night. She felt good about her skating ability, practicing turns and skating backward. She liked going backward which was her favorite skill to perform. Only now she could drive her car to the rink instead of riding the bus.

On the first day of school in September, Yvonne watched out the window as her sisters boarded the school bus. She actually shed a few tears because she could not go back to school with them. She understood for sure that a part of her life was definitely over. She realized how much she would miss seeing many of her friends as some had gone away to college, some got married, and some were working. She hardly ever saw any of them because they were busy with their new plans. She did transport her sisters to school activities occasionally, so her father did not have to take them. Of course, they rode to the skating rink with her and went shopping in town.

One night at the skating rink, Yvonne was introduced to a guy who was on leave from the Air Force, by a mutual friend, Karen. "Yvonne, this is Harry, a friend I've known through my parents. He is home on leave from the service, and asked to meet you."

She looked at Karen with apprehension and said, "Hi."

Harry smiled as he quickly replied, "Hi, glad to meet you. Would you skate with me?" So off they skated. She listened as he commented of his military life. He was good looking and appeared to be nice, but he did not excite her as Joe had. Before the night was over, he asked her to go out with him on Wednesday. She agreed to go, gave him directions to her house, and proceeded to tell Karen about their future date. Karen assured Yvonne that he was a good person as she was happy to have made a match. Yvonne was kind of glad to finally have a date, but apprehensive to go out with a total stranger.

Harry arrived at her house as planned. He was very courteous as he met her at the door, escorted her to the car, and opened the door for her. He kept the conversation simple, asking her what she liked to do besides skating. She tried to be pleasant but felt shy with him, realizing she did not feel as comfortable with him as she had with Joe. Parking the car a block from the theatre, they walked together in the warm evening air. The movie was enjoyable and Harry was pleasant, and mannerly. It really was a good date. Yvonne just did not know how she felt about this person or if she even wanted to get to know him further.

On the drive home, Harry commented, "I have four more days left on my leave. Would you go out with me again?"

She had been thinking about this possibility anyway, so she replied, "O.K. I will," accepting the date thinking it would give her a better feel for this relationship with this nice person.

As he walked her to the door of her home, he thanked her for a pleasant evening and happily said, "See you Saturday."

Again he was prompt picking her up on Saturday. He asked, "Would you mind if I took you to meet my parents?"

Yvonne realized that he was happy about meeting her, but she did not feel the same about him. She replied hesitantly, "Yes, that would be alright." After a few awkward moments at his parents' house, they left. Next, he drove to his sister's house where the family was outside on the porch. "Do you mind meeting more of my family?" He was happy as he introduced her. All were pleasant to her, but Yvonne thought it much too early to be meeting family. She was shy.

By the end of the date, she knew they would not continue this relationship. He did nothing wrong, was nice, mannerly, and kind of sweet. She just didn't feel for him the way she had with Joe. She was surprising herself how she compared him to Joe. Harry's short leave at home was over and he had to go back to the base where he was stationed. He asked if he might write to her, but she declined, for a long-distance relationship was not something she wanted to engage in again. She was pretty sure that she didn't want to proceed with this relationship any further. Yvonne wasn't sure what type of guy she wanted, but Joe had certainly given her some ideas. She made notes in her diary of the dates with Harry, but without enthusiasm.

Other new acquaintances were made at the skating rink since it was mainly the place where Yvonne, her sisters, and friends hung out. One time another guy showed up who tried to get a date with Trish. She told him, "No." Yvonne watched the interaction between Trish and this guy. She asked Trish about him, but Trish kind of blew him off like she hardly knew him. Yvonne believed her. He though, did not give up on Trish as one day he showed up at her house, trying again to get a first date with her. Yvonne wondered how he knew where she lived. His name was David, and he joined Trish and Yvonne as they shot some basketball out in Trish's driveway. Trish soon sent him away turning down another invite for a date. After he left, Trish said, "Yvonne, you should go out with him."

"No thanks," Yvonne replied, "anyway, he wants you and not me." Nothing more was said about him.

About a month later, Yvonne saw this same fellow, David, at the skating rink. He came up to her. "Do I know you?" was his silly question.

"Yes, but my friend isn't here," Yvonne answered.

"I see, but will you skate with me?" he asked.

Reluctantly, she said, "Yes." She did not know if anything more had transpired with him and Trish, but at least she knew they had never went out on a date.

Skating with him was okay, but nothing to get excited about for he wasn't so good on the skates. Trish and Yvonne had a pretty good reputation as far as being the best skaters at the rink except for the girls whose parents owned the rink.

When the night was almost over, he came up to her and asked, "Say, how about going to a movie next Friday?"

Yvonne thought she should decline his invite, but couldn't think of a good reason. "Alright," she said. "Can you find my house from Trish's?"

"Sure, I can. See you Friday about 6:00 p.m.," he replied as she went out the door.

He arrived at her house on time in a nice new white Chevrolet. Impressive! She met him at the door. Her family was scattered doing whatever, so she was not concerned about formal introductions. As he drove away from her house, he began informing her of his name and etc. "I am David Kartel, the oldest child of a large family. My father operates a dairy farm about ten miles from here. I attended high school in Howlly."

Howlly was the same town as the skating rink. His background information was good to know, but not as impressive to her as he seemed to think it was. He appeared to be a good guy, although Trish had turned him away which caused Yvonne to wonder why she had no interest in this guy. She had never asked Trish about him, in fact the mention of him never came up. He was tall, slim, blonde hair, blue eyes, and had a persistent way about him that caused one to notice him. Indeed he looked different and acted differently than any boy she had known, especially Joe.

He continued with, "I went to the university up north in Illinois for three months and then I quit because my dad needed my help on the farm which I intend to work there in the future anyway. Since my siblings are all in school, Dad and Mom have a heavy load getting all the chores done."

Yvonne thought all his information interesting and impressive, but didn't know what to comment. She nodded her head while wondering if all he said was true.

Yvonne didn't know exactly how much work it took to milk, feed, and care for the cows, but figured he was serious. "I see." She replied. "I just graduated high school in May and started working in June," she replied trying to inject her story.

As the night progressed, she thought this would probably be their only date since he seemed not impressed with her. She really couldn't blame him for not asking her out again, because she just hardly had anything to say all night. However, at the end of the night, he did kiss her, which was a surprise to her because of the way the evening had transpired. She said, "Good night," and watched as he drove away, not caring too much if she ever saw him again. She wrote of this date in her diary.

Next week, he called asking her out for a second date. Surprised at the invite, she answered, "Yes," but wondered why she did. She decided she needed to know more about him to get a better profile, and not judge him too swiftly. She hadn't learned anything negative about him, only he slightly intimidated her with his forwardness.

This second date, he drove to the city of Coltersville where they stopped at a Mexican restaurant. The building was decorated with a Spanish look, and appeared to be a very nice place. After being seated, David commented, "I met the restaurant owner's son in my short stay at college. I have eaten here several times and thought it to be a good place to bring you." She was impressed with the restaurant, food, and enjoyed the adventure.

David did most of the talking as they ordered and consumed their food. Yvonne tried hard to respond to his comments, but did not fare very well. Leading the conversation did not seem difficult for him. Talking about his family, the farm, and his plans to enjoy whatever came his way. She wasn't sure just what that included, but thought he was positive about his pursuit.

The food was delicious which she managed to enjoy even though she was nervous. David spoke to the owners, congratulating them on a fine dinner. David drove on country roads, in the direction of home. He showed her some of the farm ground which his family farmed and where some of his relatives lived.

Arriving at her house, they sat in his car for a few minutes to talk, she assumed, for it was not very late. By this time, she had learned more facts of his life and had informed him of some of her back ground. He didn't seem to be impressed by what she told him of hers. His family appeared to be financially better off than hers which left her feeling below standards.

"Thanks for the nice dinner," she commented as he moved close to kiss her.

"Yes, it is a good restaurant. I'm glad I found out about it because I do like eating there." He kissed her then and put his fingers on the buttons of her blouse.

Yvonne pulled back from him and said, "I guess I should go."

"No, it is still early, why the rush?" He kissed her again and ran his hand down her arm.

Yvonne thought he was being way too fresh and wanted to get out of the car. Her legs were shaky as she exited and stepped upon the porch of the house. David followed her and said, "Goodnight" as he kissed her again. Yvonne wondered if she should be flattered, but this much action from this stranger was too much for her. She was glad to see him leave.

As she got ready for bed, she thought about how he had kissed her several times which was surprising, for their relationship was so new. But she was distressed thinking how his hands touched her. She thought that the next time he tried that, she would stop him and then not go out with him anymore, if there even was a next time.

It was only a little more than a week, when David called for another date. Yvonne was somewhat apprehensive to accept a third date with David. Of course, she wanted to meet guys, have dates, so how else would she accomplish that if she turned down a date? He picked her up again on time in his new car, took her to another nice restaurant and then to a movie, making it a nice evening.

Always, Yvonne kept reflecting and comparing these dates with those of Joe. The dates with David were just not as much fun. *Did she always have to compare everything with Joe? Yvonne was not having such good vibes for David as she had for Joe. She even wondered why she was even on this date.* Once again they parked in front of her house as the evening grew late. He began kissing her. "Wait a minute," she whispered. *She thought she should get out of the car, away from him.* He kept on kissing her as he reached inside her blouse.

"No," Yvonne said, but he did not stop trying to feel her boobs. She pulled away from him. He pulled her back against him and pushed her down on the front seat of the car. She struggled with him, but could not get up. She kept repeating, "No." It was as if he couldn't hear, nor did he stop with his touching her. Soon he had her panties off and was upon her. "No, stop it!" she scolded, and with that it was too late. She could not get out from under him. He was strong and his weight was more than she could move. He had done something to her she had never experienced before. It hurt. Her head was pushed up against the driver's door of the car, as she felt the pressure from his movement. Yvonne felt embarrassed, hurt, and very unsure of this person she hardly knew and what he was doing to her.

Finally, he stopped moving and lay heavily upon her. She was pinned against the seat as if she were a cushion. *Now what? What does this mean? What happens next?* She was upset, scared, ashamed, and did not know what to do. *Why did he do this when she objected?* She could not move until he got off her. He said nothing, just got up and zipped his pants.

She hadn't screamed because her parents could have probably heard. Still she wondered if anyone had looked out the window and maybe saw them. She wished that she had screamed before he had gotten too far. When she was able to sit up, she buttoned her blouse with her head hanging down, totally blank as to what to say. As soon as she felt that her legs would hold her up, she got out of the car. He followed her to the door and kissed her on the cheek, saying goodnight. She could not look at him. She thought a good slap on his face was what he deserved, but she didn't react.

Quickly, she went into the house and up to her room hoping everyone was asleep. She was so embarrassed that she did not want to talk to her sisters, and she didn't want anyone to see her. She climbed into bed and cried into her pillow. Nothing like this had ever happened to her before. Joe was kind, gentle, and not aggressive. He had never once attempted to take her innocence from her. How she wished it would have been Joe instead of this person. She didn't know if she ever wanted to see him again or worse if he never wanted to see her again. She had been taken advantage of in a way no girl should have to experience. She never knew such action could happen as quickly, as rudely as this. She sobbed into her pillow, wanting to be comforted, but yet not wanting anyone to know what had transpired. Finally, exhausted, she slept.

She stayed in bed late the next morning faking sleep, wishing not to confront anyone. When she did get out of bed, she kept to herself as much as possible, hoping no one would question her of last night's date. She stayed in her room most of the day pretending to read and rest. She was afraid someone would ask her a question and she might break down and cry. She didn't know how to handle her predicament, especially with her sisters, so she avoided everyone most of that day and the next. *What would she say to them? What would be the response? They probably wondered if she was sick or something, but thankfully no one questioned her. This date and information was not written in her diary for fear her sisters might read it.*

Monday morning gave her a reprieve from family. She quickly dressed and went to work, not even speaking to her mother, who was busy doing laundry anyway. For several days, she felt confused, guilty, totally lost as to why she felt sad and bad as to what David had done to her. Never would she speak of it to anyone. Who could she trust to be able to console or advise her in this matter? She realized that her mother probably noticed her actions, yet she never questioned Yvonne. Yvonne waited anxiously to see if David would call again, almost wishing he would not.

What did this action imply to her and what did David intend by his encounter? Did this mean that he was in love with her? He never spoke any words of love. *Where does this lead? What would she do next? Should she contact him, should she never see or speak to him again?* She did not feel any love for him! Was that David's way of showing that he cared about her? She was totally confused about the whole encounter. She wished that she had never met him or gone on any date with him, certainly not the third date.

Chapter XII

David did eventually call her later next week. Yvonne didn't know if this was a good thing or not, wondering if it was in her best interest, but somehow she felt that she could not break away from him after what had transpired on the last date. It was as if the two of them had a secret from the world. At least, Yvonne never told anyone about her situation with David. He asked to see her again; she hesitantly accepted with only a small amount of courage as to what might come of this meeting. She wanted some clarity as to what transpired on the last date and how it would affect them in the future. *She was afraid to question him, but thought she deserved an explanation. Did he love her, did he really care for her, and what are his intentions?*

During his short phone call, he did not specify what they would do or where they might go. Entering his car when he arrived, he said, "We will go to my parents' house to visit with family and play cards." She made notice of each sibling, listening to conversation, and started to feel a little better being with them. Her card playing skills were barely enough to keep her in the game, as his family played often and had much skill. Her parents played card games, but she was still learning. Everyone was friendly to her and she gained an appreciation of his family as a whole. It was a pleasant evening.

Returning to her house, he parked the car on the other side of the house off the main street. He began kissing her. Yvonne thought possibly that he was beginning to like her. She timidly tried to ask him about the other night, but he was moving on quickly with his kisses and to removing her undergarment. She considered again what this could mean and thought maybe she should actually get out of the car before it was too late. This time though, he moved a little slower and was not so forceful.

Yvonne was again distressed, but thought since they had already done it once before, it wasn't such a deal to do it again. She really didn't want to experience the same thing as last time. She didn't have the courage to stop him. *Maybe,* she thought, *he really did like her.* She was relieved that there was not pain this time and David seemed to be more pleased. Yvonne didn't know what to think or how to respond. She hoped her parents didn't realize what they were doing.

Each time, she remained confused about what she and David did in the car, and kept everything a secret. They continued dating. At the end of each evening, David always parked the car near her house, and they would engage in sex, often more than just once in the same evening. Yvonne didn't know if she enjoyed doing it or not. At least, it didn't hurt like the first time. It was what David always wanted. Yvonne was scared that she might get pregnant but didn't know what to do about it.

David was always nice, took her places, but mostly they visited his relatives and family. Each night that they were together, he would want to end the evening the same way. It was always late when he would finally leave her house to go home. This routine caused her to lose out on good sleep, sometimes causing her to be grouchy and tired the next day. She began to welcome days when she would not see him so she could catch up on her rest.

After a few more weeks of the same routine, she figured they were hooked together forever. How could she ever date another guy after experiencing this kind of relationship? Love was not mentioned, nor any talk of marriage. That was alright with Yvonne, she was not ready for marriage. But still she couldn't figure out where this relationship was headed.

Instead of going out on dates, they began spending most of their time at his family farm. She went everywhere with him watching the activities as to caring for the animals, milking cows, soon realizing that his entire family had duties to perform daily, from the youngest to the oldest. Previously in her life, she had seen a cow being milked and had even tried it by hand herself on her grandfather's cow. However, this was a large operation of milking cows, all being done by machines. Yvonne stayed close to David around the farm as he did his chores. They were getting to know each other and the relationship seemed to be thriving. The whole family appeared to like Yvonne, as she was with them more often.

Several more weeks passed with basically the same pattern. This was alright with her. She liked spending time with her relatives, so why not his. She could get to know each of them this way. Then she started staying the weekend at the farm, go to church on Sunday, and then he would bring her home on Sunday evening. It all seemed to be good.

Her time at the trailer lot was somewhat boring, as there was hardly anything to do. Her sisters were busy with school and their friends. They had some time together as family, but not as it had been in years past. Anyway she got paid each week which made the car payment, kept gas in the car, and provided her a few dollars for herself. She didn't go roller skating anymore, even though she still liked skating. She was busy enough and David didn't care for the activity. The days of fall passed quickly and soon it was Christmas. David and Yvonne had gotten to know each other's family quite well. Yvonne was pleased that she and David were still dating, thinking he must like her, even maybe it was love.

David's Christmas gift to her was a total surprise as she opened the small box, as he asked her to marry him. She accepted the proposal thinking they should get married since they were engaging in the acts of marriage anyway. She could not refuse, thinking that she had nothing else going. She was delighted that he asked, for it must be that he loved her and wanted her in his life. She figured they could be a happy couple, although, she never felt the love for David that she had possessed with Joe. She thought she would get over Joe and be happy with David. She must, because the progression of their relationship had been positive, the future looked bright, and both families were in agreement (David's family more so than Yvonne's).

Much later in life, David revealed to her that he assumed they should get married because he had initiated the sex and thought they should marry. That was her reasoning for marrying him. Did she love him? Well it certainly was not the same feelings she had for Joe. But Joe was different and they had both been younger. She thought she had matured a little since her friendship with Joe. Did David really love her? He said he did, but he certainly acted very differently than the way Joe ever did with her. She thought it must be the difference in age, education, and environment.

Again, she compared him to Joe, because the relationship with Joe had been so good. She didn't smile or laugh as much with David as she had with Joe, never talked with him as she had with Joe, but then there were other good reasons for them to marry. David had a good job, he had good work ethics, was intelligent, good looking, tall, strong, and apparently wanted to share his life with her. They went to the church where his family attended, where he had attended all his life. The good points seemed to add up more than the not so good. She told herself that it was just a rough beginning.

The wedding date was set for April, by David's family, which would be before planting season started on the farm. Yvonne figured this was a bit too soon for her to prepare, but agreed. There was no way she could come up with enough money to even buy a dress, let alone pay for a wedding. David and Yvonne continued to see each other almost every evening, doing the same thing. Regardless of the activity they pursued at the beginning of the evening, they always ended with having sex, often more than just once.

After a round of sex, David would fall asleep for an hour or so, then wake up and want to do it again. It was always in the wee hours of the morning when she would creep into the house and he would dash for home. Sometimes she spent the night at his house, sleeping with his sisters in the beginning and then with David after the engagement. She didn't find this situation particularly fascinating or fun, but it seemed to be the thing David wanted. She did not write about any part of their secretive actions in her diary. The days quickly passed as did the winter months with the wedding plans coming forth.

Yvonne didn't know anything about planning a wedding or getting ready for marriage. Other girls her age got married, so she supposed she could handle it also. Actually, David's mother stepped up to take charge of the wedding with many plans of her own. Yvonne was somewhat surprised for her to want to do the planning, but decided it may be a good thing, since she lacked the knowledge of where to start. It seemed to be a very nice gesture for her to make the preparations for her son's wedding, when it appeared to Yvonne that she had so much going on in her daily routine anyway with milking cows and managing a large family. She didn't mind, even seemed to enjoy the whole process.

Yvonne was very much appreciative of her new mother-in-law's offer to take charge of so many details. Therefore, all Yvonne needed to do was to find a wedding gown, which was in itself a stressful situation because she could not afford to buy a new one. One evening she went over to her sister-in-law's, feeling quite down about this problem. "Hi, Carla, can I come in?"

"Sure, how are wedding plans coming? It is so nice that you are having a church wedding."

"I guess," she sighed, "but I don't know what to do about a gown. You know I can't afford to have one made, nor can I even afford to buy one."

"Yes, they are quite expensive."

"What am I going to do?" she asked as she almost started to cry.

Carla looked at her sadly as she had not a clue because she had been married by a Justice of the Peace. Then a light came on as she spoke, "A girl I know at work just got married, she is your size, maybe she would loan you her dress."

"Really, Carla, do you think she might?" Yvonne asked with an amazed look on her face.

"I will find out tomorrow at work," she replied.

"Oh, Carla, that would be wonderful. Thank you so much." She hugged her tightly, thinking this would be an answer to a big problem.

Carla stopped by the next evening to tell Yvonne that the girl said yes, she could borrow the gown. When Carla brought the dress to her, Yvonne could not believe how great a fit it was, as if it had been made for her. It was a very lovely gown, had a long train, a simple but lovely veil, and fit perfectly. Yvonne could not believe her lucky stars! Surely this must be a good sign. Yvonne's parents offered to pay for the flowers, and so with all that David's mother was doing, the wedding was on track for the date as planned.

The middle of March, David's mother plus a couple of his aunts hosted a bridal shower for Yvonne. It was a large party including all of David's relatives and friends and neighbors. Yvonne was overwhelmed with all the people who brought gifts for her and David to share. This was a very amazing day! Never had so many women and girls lavish so much attention on her. There were many new people, whom Yvonne was not acquainted. She had no idea how she was going to remember everyone's name. There was Aunt Bertha, Aunt Lisa, Aunt Margaret, and others, two grandmothers and a great grandmother, plus so many other cousins and friends.

She could not believe all the new items she was opening; quilts made by the grandmas, lots of new sheets, soft pretty towels, dishes, other kitchen gadgets, pillows, baking pans, and much more. She had never seen so many new essentials except in a department store. Everyone was very generous. Trying to keep it all clear in her mind of who gave what, was lost in a minute. Not to worry though, David's sister wrote down each and every gift and giver. Yvonne was amazed and grateful for everyone's generosity as she kept staring at all the gifts saying, "Thank you all." It was way more than a couple needed to start a life together.

Two weeks later, Yvonne's own grandmother and Aunt Lila also held a bridal shower for her inviting many of the relatives in her family. It was a very happy occasion with much laughter, lovely gifts, and love shared, since she had a special bond with all her aunts. Yvonne's grandma purchased a large wicker laundry basket and filled it with all kinds of spices, kitchen products, bowls, spatulas, and more. Yvonne knew it had cost a lot to fill the basket. All the attention Yvonne was receiving was very overwhelming, but graciously received. She realized how much love her family had for her in their hearts. Every aunt wished her happiness knowing how much nicer this wedding would be than what each of theirs had been.

The parties, all the gifts, well wishes from all, plus the house that was being prepared for them seemed to be a fairy tale. *Could it all be real?* Thinking about the actual day of the wedding brought to Yvonne thoughts of fear of the future, worry about the fact that this was the right decision, and a basic feeling that she was not ready to leave her family with whom she had lived with her whole life. As the wedding date got closer, the more anxious she was. Thinking about her past and how this relationship with David had begun, she wished that she could have a serious conversation with someone before she went ahead with this marriage. That person should be her mother, but they had never had such a conversation.

Explaining to her mother how David had taken advantage of her did not seem to be possible. Anyway, her mother would tell her to get married. Maybe she could talk to Carla, but she would not know what to do and she would tell Edward, which Yvonne didn't want him to know. Would Grandma be greatly disappointed in her if she knew? Any possibilities of telling someone of her worries just didn't seem to be a good idea. She figured she must live with the situation and make the best of it. Everyone thought her wedding plans were bringing her happiness. If only someone really knew all the facts and emotions, she was dealing with.

Her parents wanted the best that life could present their daughter. They had dealt with being poor their whole life, and never participated in a formal wedding ceremonial. Many weddings in her family had taken place at the court house or in the home of the family. Actually this was the first church wedding to take place for the family. Everyone was happy for her nice wedding experience.

Marriage was a very big deal to Yvonne. She did not want to let her family down by making some foolish mistake, but how could she know if this was the right thing to do? No one tried to talk her out of getting married, and since she had already had sex with David, she thought it was probably best that she get on with it. She just didn't feel real happy about the one on one relationship with her intended spouse. She kept telling herself that it was all good, that she should be satisfied with the relationship she had with David because he came from a good family and for all appearances looked as if they would have a decent life. So really, what was she worried about? She decided that it was too late now to change her mind.

Thank God it was a nice spring day as Yvonne solemnly began the day on which she was to be married. *Will any of my friends come to see me get married? How would I feel if I were marrying Joe? Never mind, can't consider that now, too late, I must move forward.* Yvonne managed to use the whole day to prepare herself for the ceremony, pausing throughout the day to reflect on her life this far. What else could she be doing or could have done? She told her sisters how pretty they looked as they left the house before she did. Once she put on the lovely white gown, she walked down the steps of her parent's house, met them at the door where her father and mother were waiting. She felt mostly scared, a little excited, a whole bunch nervous, and not very happy as she had always dreamed her wedding day would be. She assumed that her nerves kept her from feeling the happiness.

She was quite silent as they made the drive to the church. She wondered what her parents really thought about her getting married. They never really proclaimed to be very pleased or disappointed in this decision she had made. It just seemed to be the thing to do when a girl finished her education. She looked at her parents sitting in the front seat, all dressed up in their best suits. How proud she felt to be their child. *Did she want to leave them? No. It must be the time to do so.*

The rest of the wedding party and David's family were at the church, all worried that maybe she wasn't going to show because they expected her to get dressed at the church. What? Yvonne had no clue that she could have gotten dressed at the church. She did not know protocol as it was not her church and no one had mentioned it to her. Also, the photographer was busy taking pre-wedding pictures, which someone had also failed telling Yvonne about this detail. So anyway, after a few photos were taken of her with her mother, her bridesmaids, and her father, her father took her arm and stood inside the back door of the church. His big job was to walk her down the aisle.

As they took their first step, he began to cry. Yvonne didn't know what to do. *Should she stop the procession? Everyone in the church was looking at them. Should she speak to her father, maybe give him a hug and thank him for being her father? Why was he crying? The only time she had seen him cry was at the funeral of his father and brother.* In her nervous state, she just looked at him, put on a little smile, took another step forward, and continued down the aisle.

When they arrived at the front of the church, he kissed her, and took a seat beside Mom, who comforted him and told him, "It will be alright." Yvonne pondered in her mind as to what her father might be concerned about. She was his first daughter to be married, so the assumption was that he was just very emotional about giving his daughter away. The music finished playing and the minister began to speak.

The ceremony proceeded with the usual order of prayer, music, oaths, ring exchange, pledges, and acceptance. Yvonne's mind was pretty much blank, what was the music, what vowels were pledged, would she remember any of it? Everything passed so swiftly it didn't seem real. The little time from beginning to end was over. David kissed her in front of everyone, then quickly walked her down the aisle to the back of the church, where he took her in his arms and kissed her like he was really happy. *Well*, she thought, *maybe this is a good thing.* She felt so relieved that the main part was over. They both smiled as the guest exited the church. Yvonne was very pleased to hear all the nice comments and well wishes. Lots of family and friends were in attendance, flowers were beautiful, and it certainly was a beautiful day.

After everyone exited out of the church, the bride and groom then made their way through the crowd, who were now standing outside throwing rice and cheering as the couple entered the waiting car. David helped her get the white gown into the car. They waved to everyone as David's uncle drove away proceeding to the reception hall, where guest would gather for more celebration. It was a very big reception with food, dancing, laughter, opening gifts, meeting more people.

Yvonne was wowed beyond her biggest dream. Her mind was in a whirl trying to pay attention to everything going on, greeting everyone, eating, dancing, and opening gifts. There were many more wonderful gifts; a very nice set of china, silverware, silver candle holders, many sets of glasses, more sheets and towels. It was all so much more than she had ever expected. Why was she to receive so much at this time? What a big day! What an exciting night! Would she ever forget this day? Could she live up to her part of the marriage? She thought herself to not be very well qualified to be a wife, to run a home, but she would give it everything she had.

Finally, the big day was coming to a close, the dancing stopped as the music ended. Gradually, people left. Yvonne thought she might awaken to find it all to be a dream. Yvonne and David finally arrived at their new home, she was one tired puppy. David carried her over the threshold into the bedroom, but it was still a while before they slept, because David was pumped with expectations to be met. Yvonne cooperated, was very receptive to him, trying to please her new husband, although there had been no schooling or previous counseling on the part of sex for her.

There was not going to be a honeymoon because David had farm work to do starting Monday morning. Yvonne was okay with that because she knew they didn't have extra money to spend on a trip. Besides, David's parents had spent quite a bit of money on the wedding and preparing a house for them to live in. The two of them had gone shopping for furniture several weeks before and purchased a couch, two chairs, and kitchen table with six chairs, which basically gave them what they needed to set up housekeeping. The rest of the furnishings were used pieces given to them. That was it. Everything seemed to be good.

Sleeping late the next morning, David initiated sex when he woke! Finally, when hunger overtook them, Yvonne got out dishes and pans to prepare breakfast for her new husband. David's family arrived shortly after they finished eating. They all helped unload gifts from the car, checking out special items, and talking about the ceremony. Eventually, they departed, so it was more sex and sleep. *That's what marriage is about, isn't it?*

Monday morning, Yvonne and David rose quite early as his normal routine would be starting with the early morning milking and feeding the cows. David liked bacon, eggs, and toast for breakfast. So that was what she prepared. When he finished eating, he kissed her, leaving the house and traveling to the main farm place where his parents were living. This was now the first time she was totally alone in a strange house to…do what? Her first day at her own home as a wife was now here.

Yvonne walked around the large two-story farmhouse trying to decide where to put some of the wedding gifts, thinking about her future, and reflecting on how she had reached this period of her life. She opened each gift once again, carefully examined it, and put each in a place she thought proper. This was what she occupied the morning until time to prepare lunch for David.

In the next of many days, she stayed busy with organizing each room, cooking meals, and waiting for David to come home for lunch and again in the evening for dinner. She was not liking the fact that she was alone most of the day, with only David coming for lunch to break the hours of time alone. She did her best to fill each day, trying to model her new role as wife after her own mother in running the affairs of her new home, but there was not enough to keep her busy day after day. David's request for sex several times a day, was one surprise Yvonne had to adjust to. She had no idea that some people indulged so often, but it was her duty as his wife. Was it not? Yvonne often considered the idea that she might get pregnant from all this sexual activity, but would that be so awful, after all they were married and married people had babies. She did not get pregnant.

David decided he would use Yvonne's '55 Chevy to drive to and from work. Before the marriage, he lived with his parents' and did not need to drive to work. Now they lived a half mile from the farm so he needed to drive to where all the farm activity took place. Yvonne had the availability of his car to drive if she needed to go to the grocery store or anywhere. This seemed fair to Yvonne. Little did she realize that he would be entering the car with dirty clothes and muddy work boots. Besides the dirt, the car soon showed wear and a few dings and scratches. What was he doing with her car? She did not complain to him about it, but it hurt her pride because it was her first car. It was such a big step in her life to purchase her personal vehicle. Now to see it in this kind of shape was heart-wrenching.

But that was not the worst of it. David tried driving it throughout the winter without adding antifreeze, so the block cracked, and that was how her first car met its end. David had it hauled away and he purchased himself a pickup truck, which was what he wanted anyway. It did not bother David in the least as to what he had done to her car. Yvonne felt a sadness to realize how something so precious to her in the beginning, had been destroyed in such a careless way. She made no comment about it though, because she still had a vehicle to drive and David had a pickup. Was that not progress?

Chapter XIII

Each day began almost the same way, bacon and eggs for breakfast. Bacon was fried a few pieces at a time in an iron skillet, and then eggs were dropped into the hot grease. It was messy and could be dangerous. This early routine required some effort from Yvonne, which was hard for her to adjust, but she did it. She tried very hard to be a good wife, cook, and housekeeper. Cooking was not a new activity for her, but she thought there was still a lot to learn preparing more elaborate meals.

It seemed that David's mother could cook everything and all of it tasted delicious. She explored the cookbook given to her by her grandmother, and tried to improve her meals following recipes in the book. She modeled her actions after her own mother and aunts, which she thought would be effective and pleasing to her husband. Little did she know what he wanted from her as his lover, his wife. Her shyness and insecurity hampered her attempts to fulfill some actions. Figuring how to act to get David to give her the love and attention she desired, was a problem. She assumed that he loved her, sometimes said that he loved her, but somehow she didn't get the feel good kind of love from him that she wanted. He never told her that she was pretty, so she assumed that she wasn't. After all, his sisters participated in beauty pageants. Compared to them, she fell short, at least in her mind and David's opinion. These little nuances lodged in her mind, but she said nothing about them to anyone. The romance that she was looking for was just not available.

The first several of months of her new marriage, she was home alone trying to stay busy with whatever she could think of doing. These days became quite lonely for her, since previously she had always been with her sisters and family. Once in a while, she would visit her mother, but with her sisters in school, the home life she knew was no longer available. Her past had consisted of family, school, band, etc.; now all that was over.

Trying to overcome this loneliness and the lack of activity, she decided to get more involved in the farm with her husband and in-laws. What could it possibly harm if she were to hang around the milking parlor at the main grounds where the most activity was happening? The rest of David's family was totally involved, so why couldn't she be allowed to participate also? She used to hang out with David before they were married, so why not now.

One afternoon, she mustered the courage to appear at the milking parlor, to watch and be with people. Most everyone seemed surprised to see her arrive, yet also expressed gratitude that she had decided to join the activity. This welcoming was a good feeling for Yvonne. There was casual conversation and plenty of information on how to deal with the cows. Quickly, opportunities opened up where she realized that she could lend a hand.

This was a day that so changed her daily, boring, routine and began for her a new life on the farm with her husband and his family. Each day she showed up at milking time. She took in all the information given her and soon learned all about the process from beginning to the cleaning up of the milking parlor. She could tell that David was pleased with her getting involved in the farm. David immediately expected her to continue helping, which she didn't mind because it used a good part of her day, and therefore, she was not lonely. One thing she did not think about, was that very soon, David thought she should help with the milking twice daily, morning and afternoon. She agreed to do this even though it was very difficult to rise so early every morning.

David soon decided that her next lesson was to drive a tractor. She had ridden on the tractors with him, so she had a good idea of what it took to handle such equipment. David began, "This is the clutch here on the left side, the brakes are on the right. There is a left brake for left turns and a right brake for right turns. Got that?" She nodded her head. "You know how the gear shift works, right? This lever is for the gas to the motor. Now, put the clutch in and start the motor." She did.

"Slowly, let out the clutch to start moving." She did just as he instructed and the tractor began to move. She drove down through the pasture and turned around as per his direction. Thus began her first day of driving a tractor and defined her as a worker on the farm.

She was not following her husband around on the farm any more. She was doing chores assigned to her, filling in where ever needed. She learned all aspects such as how to bed the cows, feed the baby calves, and to give them all plenty of hay to munch on. This became her daily life. Farming was a very good and rewarding profession in which she was glad to be a part of. There was some satisfaction in that each time a job was completed, you could see the results. Besides you were helping to feed other people all over the world. Being outdoors was another factor of farming which she enjoyed versus staying indoors all day. So now most days she was quite busy doing her assigned chores and still doing her housework and cooking, which was alright with Yvonne because it all made each day more fulfilling.

She felt more a part of a team with David and more a part of the family as she did her share of the farm chores. When it came time for making hay, David decided that Yvonne could drive the tractor that pulled the baler, which pulled a wagon on which he rode to stack the bales of hay. It was easy enough, just follow the row of hay, go slow, make gentle turns, and do not make a quick stop. She did this with ease and caution as David directed. She was pleased with her ability to do these chores making her a part of something bigger.

With all the time and effort Yvonne put into farming, David, in turn, never offered assistance with helping her in the house. Yvonne knew that some men did not help their wives, but she really wished that he would. It had been her decision to start helping on the farm and she was not sorry of that, so she would still do chores and still cook and clean and whatever else a wife had to do. It was the farm way, was it not?

All work and no play makes for a dull life, as they say. Entertainment consisted of going to a relative or friend's house to play cards, have snacks, and talk. Many times, the relatives or friends came to their house. It was good to do this type of entertaining versus spending money on traveling to a movie or restaurant. When folks were invited to their home, Yvonne had to clean the house, make sandwiches of some type, and bake a cake or pie for the guest. "Be the hostess with the most talent, and then clean everything up the next day after the party was over." David would arrive at the party, enjoy himself, drink too much, and be off to work the next morning. Oh well, so this is her life. Some days you win, some days are more like losing.

This new way of living, was challenging, fulfilling, and physically exhausting. She felt obligated to complete all chores assigned to her as she thought she was now a part of the farm. Yvonne thought her marriage was working as well as many others. She often wondered, though, *where is the happiness*? Some days were better than others, even a little fun, but not the 'Happy Ever After Days' type of life written in books, or in a movie.

Actually being on the farm, in the mist of all the activity, Yvonne quickly surmised that much of the talk was about sex. One had to know when it was time to breed a heifer or cow, make arrangements to put her in the pen with the bull so he could perform his duty, and when time came for the arrival of the calf, sometimes one had to assist the heifer in the birthing process. Children on the farm, learned at a very early age about sex. This was normal procedure to them. Animals had to reproduce to replace the aging cow to keep the herd vital.

The big conversation was about the bull. Boy, did he ever have the good life! All he had to do was to eat, sleep, and wait for a female to be brought to him to be serviced. One day David came into the milking parlor and said, "Yvonne, come help me put this heifer in with the bull." This was one of David's duties, which he enjoyed being the one to present the bull with a partner. He would then watch and root for the bull as the as he did his duty. The poor heifer had to support the weight of the massive bull while he made his maneuver. This action instilled in David the desire to live such a life as the bull.

At least now, Yvonne understood some of his excitement for sex, but thought humans should conduct themselves in a more loving, tender way toward their mate. Maybe somehow she could convey this message to him. She would try to do that.

Two years of marriage and working on the farm was good. Yet, Yvonne thought maybe it was time for David and her to become parents. Finding the courage to speak to David about trying to begin a family, became a goal for her. Oh yes, the trying part is what got his attention. He agreed that it might be nice to start a family although he didn't seem too sincere about it. She tossed the matter two ways in her mind; maybe they should wait longer until they had better financing. When would that be? Maybe they needed to be more mature to handle the most important position in the world. Still other young couples had started a family, so why not the two of them? Sexual cohabitation was always plentiful in their daily routine. So, really, why was she not getting pregnant?

As they lived their daily lives on the farm, America was involved in fighting in some foreign country of which Yvonne understood very little about. She realized that some of her former classmates had enlisted in the service and were now away from their families fighting in a country of which she knew nothing. Yvonne considered the lives of her cousins and other friends who were at this time serving in the military and possibly how some of these men might not return home, or even be able to start a family, or be here to raise their children if they already had any. That information greatly weighed on her mind and impressed on her even more the thought of wanting to have a family of her own. The more she thought about it the more she wanted to have a baby. It didn't happen right away, but finally, she became pregnant.

When she left the doctor's office with the news, Yvonne was excited, but yet concerned as to how she would handle motherhood. She carried the excitement and fears in her heart, sincerely treasuring the child within her. David was somewhat excited about the news of the pregnancy in that he had made it possible. *Was he truly happy knowing that he would soon become a father? He was not attentive of her condition, nor did it make any difference as to her household chores. At least, most of the farm chores which she had been doing were taken off her to-do list.*

Pregnancy was a whole new experience for her. She embraced the thought of having a new-born baby to love, hold, and treasure, but she knew nothing of the growth and process of getting to the birth. As a youngster, she had seen her aunts pregnant and then a short time later, a new born baby would be introduced to the family. She was not aware of the physical changes to take place in her body except gaining weight from a baby bump. It was only a few weeks into the pregnancy when she got sick in the morning.

This was the first time of many mornings for about three or four months. She was not actually sick at these times, just could not keep some foods in her stomach. This was just an inconvenience because she only had a moment's notice for when she might upchuck. She did not like this phase of pregnancy but accepted this problem as normal and dealt with it when it happened and moved on. The rest of the nine months went fairly smoothly except for the inconvenience of not being able to bend over or lift something heavy.

Considering all aspects of the pregnancy, she felt good, pleased with it, and could hardly wait for the arrival. The thought of life forming inside her body totally amazed her. She was surprised of her weight gain and shape her body was taking, but still marveled at the process.

Early in the year before their third anniversary, a baby girl arrived. Yvonne couldn't have been more pleased with this newborn, the most beautiful baby she had ever seen. She was fascinated by her beauty and awed by the fact that she absolutely had a part in producing this beautiful little child. She loved her and bonded immediately. *But what was up with David?* She noticed how he seemed so detached to the whole process of their child's birth and welcoming their new one. Other family members noticed his lack of enthusiasm, suggesting that David was disappointed because the baby was a girl instead of a boy. They thought he would have been happier with a son for his firstborn child.

Well, it was not Yvonne's fault that they had a girl, was it? How petty! Yvonne loved her beautiful baby and was thrilled with being the one to have total charge of a wonderful new life, naming her Dolly because she absolutely was a doll. She fed her, cuddled her, and loved her more than anything in the world. David did not even try to cuddle the baby, nor was there any pride in him as a new father. Yvonne thought this was strange and unacceptable for him to behave as he did.

What with all the younger siblings he had, his family excused his behavior feigning that he thought another baby was just that, another baby. The same way a cow had another calf every year. But her baby was not just another calf, she was human, a very dear part of herself. She wanted to have a child, now she had a precious one. What a wonderful experience for Yvonne to have, to remember, to cherish her whole life.

As Dolly grew, David exemplified minor fatherly bonding with her. *How could he be so resistant?* Yvonne was still concerned and confused with him. He had agreed to begin their family, now why didn't he participate as a father should? She had imagined that the two of them would be happy, proud, and very good parents. She went about her chores caring for Dolly like the mother she aspired to be.

The one thing David continued was the amount of sexual activity with Yvonne. As long as Yvonne cooperated in this area of his desire, he was pretty much alright to live with. Then, before Dolly was even one year old, Yvonne went to the doctor for a checkup and found out that again she was pregnant. What? Not yet! She was enjoying her first baby so much, that she wasn't quite ready to deal with another. David was only pleased in that he had produced the pregnancy. She did not understand his attitude about sex, love, responsibility, and family.

It had taken her some time to get pregnant the first time, so this second time was certainly not expected, especially so soon. It took her a few weeks to accept this news thinking how she wanted a family, so now it had become a reality. *Why so soon? What is the rush?* She kept trying to find a balance to this prevalent situation.

Once again, this pregnancy progressed much the same as the first. She had morning sickness again, which was a bit more of an inconvenience because she had Dolly to tend to. She tolerated the condition and managed to get through the few months that it lasted. It was a bit more of a strain to be pregnant and do her household chores and care for the first baby, but women had managed to do it for years, nothing new.

Time passed quickly as Yvonne and Dolly got into routine of daily chores. In the middle of a very hot summer, after a tiring day of making apple pies, a boy rushed in to join their family. Now surely David would be pleased and they could be a happy family. He seemed to be satisfied, but other than showing pride for a son, his love for the children was not as apparent as Yvonne had envisioned it would from a good father. Yvonne learned to live with his attitude, but no way could she understand. She tried to involve him to be more a part of the family by asking him to join in the play with them. That was only sporadic. Her two little ones filled her days and nights. She loved her babies and supplied their every need the best she knew how. She thought that there was nothing better to be in this world than a 'mother'.

Yvonne was not a demanding person, never asked for much. Her parents had always taught their children to be thankful for food, clothing, and home. To ask or expect more than that was about being selfish. Yvonne did the housework, cleaning, cooking, and caring for the babies 24/7 besides still pleasing David, taking care of his wants and needs. Only a few months in the spring and in the fall, Yvonne helped with the farm chores by driving a tractor to disc a field or run the baler. It was physically tiring to drive tractor all day, bathe the children for bed, and take care of laundry such as was needed.

She did all she could each day without much complaint, but thought David expected a little too much of her since they had two little ones. This made her days long and hard, but she managed to do what was necessary. David was not helping with feeding the children, bathing them, or tucking them into bed. She had to do it all. And then before she had even considered the possibility of being pregnant again, she was. *Oh my goodness!* How could she handle anymore chores in her day? Yes, she very much wanted a child to start a family, but this would be more than she had bargained for. It was overwhelming for her to think about three little children, all the housework involved, David's needs, and the need to be strong for all involved. She prayed, "Lord, I asked for a baby, now I will have three. How will I be able to handle it?"

It took all her energy to be mother, housemaid, cook, and wife. This all became a strain on her strength and nerves. Her body was worn down with producing babies, and doing the physical jobs around the house to provide for all. Problems also developed as David was still insistent on his 'time' with Yvonne. He was not concerned how tired she might be. She never complained to him about his lack of help around the house, but wished that he would pitch in.

Then came a time when David got angry with her complaining about her poor efforts in being a good wife. She spent too much time with the children, she allowed them to play with their toys anywhere, and she was always too busy to sit with him. He found a notebook in which Yvonne kept track of her spending of household expenses, which enraged him. He stormed through the house yelling, "What are you trying to do? Do you want people think I am not a good provider? Why would you do this?"

She was shaking as the words squeaked out, "No, no, I just wanted to make sure I didn't spend too much on trivial things. I was only checking myself to see how I was spending."

He threw the book at her and stomped out of the house yelling, "You are so inconsiderate of everything I do."

Yvonne continued crying, failing to understand his anger. She consoled the children as she slowly regained her composer. There were other episodes in which he became angry with her when she least expected it. Yvonne never knew when he might attack her with some foolish complaint. Her nerves were strained day after day as she did her best to please him. She loved her children tremendously and enjoyed their little antics while David couldn't understand why their toys had to be spread about the rooms yet, he never made any attempt to pick any of them up. There were angry moments, complaints from him of her not being a good wife, and sometimes, talk of divorce.

Yvonne didn't know how she could continue. On days when they visited her parents, she kept up a good front pretending all was well, when she actually wanted to talk to someone about her disappointment of her marriage. Still, she really didn't want her parents to know how unhappy she was. She thought they probably surmised it anyway.

Three years passed with counseling from their minister. This counseling helped the situation some. The preacher's advice of being nice to each other, helpful and appreciative, only went so far. As their daily routine became more settled, Yvonne thought maybe they had overcome the more difficult years of marriage and perhaps the future would be a little better. They had been married nine years now, which seemed to be an accomplishment of some degree. Her burden of chores became a little lighter now that the little ones had outgrown diapers and could get around of their own power. Still, it took constant watch of them for protection and teaching. Yvonne didn't mind watching, hovering, and playing with them. It took more consecrated effort to please David to keep him on an even keel.

It was very unnerving to even think of having another child, but they concluded that one more would be a nice number of four, and if it were a boy, so much the better! She wasn't completely sold on this plan, but figured another boy would even the score, and perhaps give David more pride. She hoped and prayed this would be the result. One day she realized that she was pregnant with baby number four. Thank God the fourth child was a son. What a nice family she had been blessed with. What more could a girl ask for? Life seemed to be fairly pleasant for a while. Yvonne was able to handle the new little one and attend to the other three. Actually, Dolly was quite her mother's helper.

David and Yvonne had beautiful children, a nice home, food, and enough money to pay the bills. Yvonne was thrifty as she had learned from her mother and never spent money for things they couldn't afford. Still, they had situations in which David would always seem to find something to complain about. She tried hard to keep peace in the house, to please him, to keep the little ones healthy and happy. Gradually, it seemed that David had slipped back into his old complaints.

A couple of times when he got angry about something, he would push Yvonne, sometimes knocking her down to the ground. He would pick her up and throw her onto the bed. The children would get frightened and hide. Yvonne was no match for him with his size and strength. What was she to do? When he calmed down, they would have sex and then she would tread very carefully to not anger him again, if only she could understand why.

Another time, David got very angry with Yvonne. "Why on earth do you act like that? You cause embarrassment to my family." He growled at her as they left a birthday party.

She spoke not a word for fear of what he might do. They got into the car, he started it, and sped out of the parking lot. She feared the ride home and whatever else he might do to her. As she tried to escape from his reach, he struck her across the mouth. Afraid of what else he might do to her, she sat quietly on the ride home. It was a night of fear, heart break, and tears for all the pain he had caused her over the years. Thank God, the children were spending the night with her mother. Yvonne had had enough of his bullying and was ready to call it quits for good. She didn't know what to do or where to begin her course of action, but she had made up her mind to take a stand for herself.

Of course, the next morning, David was sorry, begged her forgiveness, and tried to convince her that all would be good. She listened to his pleadings and pitiful excuses. He was sorry that he lost his temper and acted in a bad way, but claimed he still wanted her and the children. Yvonne had trouble believing him; that he would be good to her, that he would not harm her; and that he would learn to be a better husband and father. She listened with much doubt and then agreed to try again to be a family, on condition that they both undertook some full-fledged counseling. He complied.

They did counseling in a more professional system. During this time, they were very tolerant of each other as they went about their daily routine. At first, Yvonne didn't see how this counseling was going to change their lives any more than the one before. She kept going and hoping that things would improve. Yvonne thought she was learning some good ideas for improving her self-confidence and trying to talk to David more in a constructive way.

David obliged, going to the sessions for about three months and then quit. He said none of that stuff applied to him. This frightened Yvonne as she thought he was quitting way too soon for all the issues to be resolved. She really wanted all her misery and pain to be gone. She continued with the counseling despite his lack of willingness. She wanted desperately to feel better about herself as a wife, mother, and individual. At least, he wasn't getting angry as he used to. He wasn't acting so badly as before. As she became stronger from the lessons that she learned, they were able to work out some of their problems. They kept trying to work together on everything until they had figured a way to live a better day to day life.

With their marriage held together with paper and glue, David decided that farming with his parents and family was getting too involved with too many people as his sisters married. He had put his whole life and soul into this farm and thought he should not have to share with all of them. So he began looking for some acreage which he could farm and make a living for his own family. Yvonne supported this decision, having good thoughts of being on their own. He found a house with acreage which he thought would be enough for him to manage. Yvonne was pleased with the new house and area in which they would be living. The two of them made the move with little help from anyone else.

David took on a whole new perspective. He had a plan, put it to work, and settled his family into a new chapter of life. David and Yvonne worked together getting set up to farm the ground they had acquired. Yvonne liked the idea that they now operated a farm belonging only to them. Life seemed to be a good deal better. David seemed to be calmer each day as he and Yvonne worked together. Yvonne organized the house, instructed the children of new rules for living on their new farm. They all loved it. Life was better the way the two of them worked together to prepare the ground, plant crops, and share in all the responsibilities on their property. There wasn't near as much work to be done, so the two of them could handle all chores each day without a lot of effort.

Their social life developed much differently. The new friends they met at church were very similar in age, family size, and farming background. It was nice to be a part of a group sharing the same goals. They did not visit with relatives anymore, seeing them only occasionally. It was not necessary for his family to be involved with their lives. Most of his family was not agreeable to the split of David's leaving, but it was done. He was determined to make the best of this property, farming it the best he knew.

The children grew, attended school, and changes came about as to the work load on Yvonne. It seemed to her that maybe all the bad stuff was behind them. There was no more complaining from David, and Yvonne was able to manage the household chores and still be able to assist David in ways he needed. It seemed as if their problems were just a ghost of the past. And so, for almost two years, life was better, even good. This was more of what she had always thought a family should be, David and Yvonne working together. There was not as much to do on their small farm, as there was on the bigger farm with his family.

This new stage of their lives was definitely better than in the troubling previous years.

Chapter XIV

Spring, 30 April 1975, began as a warm sunny day. The yard needed cleaning of sticks and debris, and preparation for the garden was in order. Yvonne got the children up and ready for school. After the three older children boarded the bus at the end of the lane, she placed young Jacob in the car and proceeded to town to pick up some groceries. David had gone out to the shed to work on a piece of equipment. Today, things felt good, at least promising to be a good day. The grocery shopping did not take much time, so she returned home before noon. After parking the car and helping Jacob out, David met her at the door with a packed bag in his hand. She looked puzzled as he spoke, "I am leaving because I can't do this anymore."

Yvonne looked at him in disbelief as she said, "What do you mean you can't do this anymore? Do what?"

"I mean that I can't live like this. I have to leave," he replied.

"Leave? Why? What is wrong?" she asked as she tried to make sense of what he was saying.

"I don't know, I just have to go." He answered as he got into the truck and drove away. She just stood there in the driveway watching him leave, her heart pounding, her mind racing. She thought what in the world had gotten into him and what was he doing? After all those years of hassle, all the time in counseling and the progress they were making, she could not make sense of what he said. She thought that they were doing so well with the farm, children, finances, and even their relationship. She could not imagine why he said that he couldn't do this anymore and why, now he was leaving. Couldn't he give her a better explanation for this sudden announcement?

Just like that he was gone, leaving her confused and in a state of shock as to what he might be going to do. They had been married almost twelve years. Yes, it had been a tumultuous twelve years, but she had survived. They had done okay financially, nothing big or fancy, but their moderate way of living was suitable. He had not been the man she wished he could have been and evidently she was not the woman he desired. She went over and over in her mind as to what could have produced this ridiculous announcement. She could not understand what he was doing.

She realized that they had never reached a real loving relationship as neither of them truly lost themselves in and of each other. So Yvonne could only conclude that he might be making a foolish mistake. He never left her a phone number or address where he could be reached, nor did he say when he would contact her.

She stumbled through the rest of the day, not able to accomplish much. As the children returned home from school, she worried more that he really might not come back. The children were not concerned about where their father might be, for it was not unusual for him to be out on the tractor, or shed, or at the neighbors. In a daze, she went about preparing the evening meal trying to act as if nothing unusual was happening. Jesse spoke first, "When will Daddy be home?"

"Sometime later," was her reply, "I think he went to help Uncle Don." As the evening passed, she kept thinking she would hear from him, maybe he would return or at least call. As she prepared the children for bed, Dolly asked, "Shouldn't Daddy be home by now?"

"Do not worry, you will see him soon." She waited up late into the night hoping to hear from him. Finally, she went to the empty bed.

He did return the next day to tell her he had contacted a lawyer and was going to start the proceedings for a divorce. He said, "I will get some more of my stuff when I know where I will be staying. You can stay here in the house and have the car. I just don't want to be married anymore."

Yvonne pleaded with him, "Please, don't do this." She tried with tears in her eyes to convince him to stay. "Please, please stay for the children. I thought we were doing so much better."

"We are," he said, "but this is not what I want."

"Well, I don't understand, what do you want?" she asked.

"Never mind, Yvonne, I am done. I will bring you papers to sign when they are ready."

Once again, he left her standing as he drove away. This was situation was unbelievable, after so many years of tears, fears, and even gradual improvements. She didn't know who to call or what she might say to them. She just stayed home as much as possible to wait this out. It was only a few weeks later when he brought her divorce papers to sign. "I can't sign this," she told him. "I need more time." She was hoping more time would give him a chance to think it over, as she certainly needed to think about a divorce. She needed time and help to figure out what was going on. She still wasn't able to figure out why David had left and was now insisting on a divorce. How could he ever leave his children? Perhaps, in a few more days, he might realize this is a mistake.

"Sure you can look it over, but I am not changing my mind," he said as he looked down on her as if she might be a lame duck.

"Do you realize how upset the children are? How they keep asking questions about you that I can't answer. You need to have a talk with them to explain your actions. I am not doing it for you."

David sat down with the children, telling them some sad story about how he needed to change his life, and how he would not be living with them anymore. Dolly sobbed, Jesse and Sissy looked on without much emotion, and little Jacob sat on his lap and sucked his thumb. Dolly hugged her daddy and cried, "Don't leave, Daddy, I don't want you to go." He hugged each one and hurried out the door without speaking to Yvonne. Yvonne did her best to console each of the children even though she was having a hard time understanding all this.

Yvonne knew nothing about what to expect in a divorce. She didn't know a lawyer, and really didn't want to talk to any. After searching the phone book and debating what she would do, she contacted a lawyer to have him look over the papers of the divorce. Upon meeting with the lawyer, his proclamation was that he could not represent her for he apparently knew some of David's family. Now what would she do? This was too much to accept. She just gave up trying to consult with a lawyer and decided to sign the stupid divorce papers. She was scared to death about what would happen to her and the children for she had not worked out of the house since they had married. What kind of job would she be able to attain? She didn't know how she would care for the children and herself.

In the divorce settlement, Yvonne and the children were to live in the house as long as she never remarried, and have all the furnishings and the car and receive a small amount of monthly support from David. That was fine, but she knew that what he offered was not enough to cover all the cost she would have raising the children. That was all he would agree to at this time. She didn't know what else to do, how to fight him, where to get help, or who might be able to guide her in this difficult decision making time.

The people and area were too new to her to involve anyone. She was too humiliated to subject her own family to this divorce process. She was too upset, confused, lost to figure out anything else to do. That was all there was to it. Her marriage had come to an end. Now, she had to tell her parents, face her friends, and try to pick up the pieces. How did she manage to climb this mountain only to roll all the way to the bottom?

Days were passing quickly. Yvonne struggled to get up each day, prepare meals, dress the children, and keep motivated. Her low confidence from so much struggle, left her thinking she was not a very strong person. The only thing which kept her going was the needs of the children. She did realize her responsibility for them. What she didn't know now or before her marriage was who she really was and what she wanted in life.

She didn't know that focusing on two people as a couple doesn't get you anywhere-the whole is only as strong as the parts. She had allowed someone to make decisions for her which gave away her power as a person. Some circumstances are not changeable, but choosing how to act in each circumstance is very important. Her self-value wasn't at a high when she met David, and only sunk lower each year she was with him. She had allowed David too much control and even when she had made a decision, it usually did not turn out very well. She, of course, did not see or know any of this as she continued to struggle each day.

Soon, the news was out. In fact, the neighborhood probably knew what was transpiring before Yvonne. For one thing, they were not in attendance at church. The word spread, and soon Yvonne found out that David was involved with a neighbor lady. In fact, she was one of Yvonne's new friends. Ouch! Life can be so cruel. *How could he do this after all she had done for him and with him? How could he just walk away?* She spent many a night crying about her dilemma, struggling each day to be strong, and trying to figure out what to do next. Big changes had to take place in her life.

Gaining strength and thinking things through as clear as she possibly could, Yvonne started making plans for a new life structure, which included caring for the children. She managed to acquire a job. Actually, she begged for this job until she was hired. Once hired for a position, she put herself in motion to make each day better for her and the children. Their daily routine took on a new way of living for them. With the three older children in school, she found a sitter for the baby where she could drop him off on her way to work each day. This was a start for her new journey as a single mom.

Everything was new to her each morning as she left the house. She had often wished that she had stayed single longer and worked for a longer time, allowing herself time to support herself and live on her own. It definitely was too late to do that. Now she had to work and care for children while living on her own. Her mother had managed for years with her father out on the road so much, somehow, she would too. She and the children grew under a new set of rules for Mom and toddlers.

Yvonne had never imagined raising four children on her own as her vision included the fact that she was supposed to grow up, get married, have children, and care for a family with her husband. What happened?

Part III

Chapter XV

Sleeping alone was very strange after many years of marriage. One gets accustomed to sharing the bed and everything in the house. When she couldn't sleep, she reminisced about all the things in her life; growing up as a girl in a large family, school days, other male friends in her past, which she had known only a few, with the exception of her brothers and cousins. She replayed episodes of her life most every night except on the nights she was too exhausted to keep her eyelids open.

Her present situation of being a single parent, and how her marriage had failed were always foremost in her thoughts. She wondered how she could have acted differently to prevent this tragedy, and was always trying to figure out why David just gave up on her and the children. She prayed a lot for God to sustain her throughout the coming days. It was too perplexing. David was too complex.

One night she thought of her past before her marriage when she knew Joe. How long had it been since she had seen or talked to him, or even thought about him? Where was he? Did he marry? Surely he did. How many children does he have? What might he be doing at this time of his life?

Daily duties for her job position were easy as the work she performed stemmed from her experience of different chores she had performed in daily living. She became stronger as each day passed. Meeting new people at work and being able to do each task well, gradually promoted new confidence in her, and the new life she now was living. David took the children every other weekend, which gave her plenty of time to catch up on whatever chores needing to be done at home. Those weekends were also horrific for her because of the emptiness of the house. She often cried the whole time the children were gone. She could not wait for Sunday afternoon when they would return to her. They were her life, her everything.

The ladies and men at church were a great comfort to her with support and kindness, always checking that she and the children were doing well. One Sunday in August, it was announced at church of an upcoming marriage to be held in the church, which all members were invited to attend. Yvonne learned that a young girl from the congregation was to marry a cousin to Joe Small. What a surprise! Curiously, she wondered who from Joe's family might be in attendance at the wedding. Maybe Joe's parents or possibly Joe himself might be present. Since Joe's parents would most likely be there, she could at least find out something about Joe. This could be a good thing or not. One never knew how the wind might blow. She debated for weeks whether she should go. What could it possibly harm? The children would be with their father, she had nothing else to do.

When the day of the wedding arrived, Yvonne put on the best dress she possessed, looked in the mirror, and asked, is this the right thing to do? She drove to the church, nervously walked through the door, and took a seat as far back as possible to get a view of who might be there that she would know. Some of the other ladies of the church sat with her. She spotted Joe's mother and father, sister, and younger brother. Yvonne was very happy to see all of them, especially Joe's mother. She knew she would have the courage to talk to her. At the reception, she approached Mrs. Small ever so shyly. "Hello Mrs. Small, I am happy to see you."

"Hello to you, Yvonne, nice to see you too," she replied. "I am quite surprised to see you here."

"Well, the whole church got invited, so that is the reason." The conversation continued with Yvonne explaining how she had been married, which produced four children, and was recently divorced.

Mrs. Small told Yvonne that Joe had also been recently divorced, that he had a daughter and a son from that marriage. It was all so surreal to be talking to Mrs. Small in such a calm, casual manner. It was very nice. When Yvonne decided to end the conversation, she suggested to Mrs. Small, "Tell Joe hello."

"I certainly will tell him and he will be very glad to hear about you," replied Mrs. Small.

She did not stay very long, feeling lost in all the joy, excitement, and people. Yvonne was pleased with how the night had progressed, especially the conversation with Mrs. Small. She had no idea if anything would come of this conversation, although she was pretty sure that Joe would receive her message from his mother. She found it ironic that Joe was single at this same time as she.

At home alone for the rest of the night, she reminisced about Joe and their past relationship. It had been a very long time since she had thought about him. She wondered if he might even be interested to see her. She would not blame him if he did not want to see her, because of all the rejection she gave him, and the way she wrote him the 'dear john' letter to say goodbye. Why had she done that?

Now, she wondered about her actions as a foolish young girl. Had she done the right thing at the time? But why hadn't she tried to contact him again after graduation? Why didn't Joe try to contact her again? Oh well, that was too many years ago, now she would have to live with reality. Anyway, she could hope that he might be willing to forgive her and give her another chance. Would that be possible?

About a week later, Yvonne answered the telephone and could not believe the voice she was hearing. "Hello, Yvonne, this is Joe." She was shocked and could hardly speak. Her wish was to hear from Joe, but thought it was unlikely, and had not figured out what she was going to say to him if he did. This was the most exciting and best phone call she had received in many years, like when Joe used to surprise her with a call so many years ago.

She smiled as she answered, "Hi, Joe, I am so surprised to hear from you. I guess your mom gave you my message."

"She certainly did." He chuckled as he spoke. "My God, how are you? Mom said you looked great and would like for me to call, so I am."

"Yes, I did, but I didn't know if you would answer my request. It is great to hear your voice." She was super nervous. How could she possibly keep up this conversation? Not to worry, because Joe was just as excited to hear from Yvonne as she was from him. They talked like they had only been apart a few months, as they exchanged their information about jobs, children, and where they lived.

Then, Joe asked, "Do you think we could meet perhaps at a restaurant in a couple of days?"

"Yes, that would be great. There is a nice fast food place at the stoplight in Hilltown. I would be happy to see you."

"That would be great," he replied. "See you then. I can hardly wait."

Yvonne was shaking as she hung up the phone, actually afraid she might wake up to find it all a dream. Did she really talk to Joe after all these years? Wow! This was so not believable! The rest of the day, her thoughts were all about Joe, how he might look, how would he respond to her now, considering how they had parted, and what if he could not forgive her for how she had rejected him in the past?

Anyway, he certainly did not sound even the tiniest bit upset on the phone. Soon they would meet in person and perhaps their feelings would be more evident. So much new activity giving her much more to worry about; how their reunion would be, what to wear, what to say to him, and how to explain why she had broken off their relationship so many years ago? Could she really give a better reason than the one she had presented him in the letter? It had been the truth. As the day of their meeting approached, she became more anxious and more excited thinking about meeting Joe. Arrangements had been made for the care of the children, so she hoped she was ready.

The set day arrived, even though Yvonne couldn't believe it was happening. She drove uptown to the restaurant when she left work, which only took ten minutes. She was getting more nervous by the minute. In her mind, she recalled the day of her seventeenth birthday and how she had purposely ridden the bicycle to her cousin's house to meet Joe.

It had worked so well back then, but now she wondered if she would be so lucky at a second chance. She thought that arriving early, she would have a little time to calm her nerves and maybe get a peek of Joe before he saw her. As she pulled into the parking lot, there was already a semi-truck parked on the other side of the lot, which could possibly be the one Joe would be driving. She nervously exited the car, keeping her eyes on the truck. The man exited the truck and stood beside the tractor trailer, then began walking toward her. He looked directly at her and she knew it was him. Wow! She had the urge to run into his arms, but thought that may be a little brash.

After all these years, he was still very good-looking. It made her shiver to think how long it had been since she had last seen him. He smiled at her and welcomed her into his arms. How comforting it felt to be hugged by someone she had loved so many years ago! All the good feelings, safety, and even love enveloped her as they embraced. It seemed as though they had only been apart for a very little time. How could all the good feelings from the past survive? What had they been missing all those years? He was maybe two inches taller and about twenty-five pounds heavier than he had been last time she had seen him. His beautiful black hair was just as fabulous as before, plus a mustache produced a very manly look. Wow, he possibly could have been fat and bald! Yvonne couldn't have been more pleased with his looks, with this meeting.

Joe also was very nervous but eager to greet Yvonne, for his love for her had never died. He felt such happiness in his heart, more than he ever thought could ever be possible. He was worried, too, about how this meeting could go wrong, remembering the past with a touch of the hurt from her rejections. For now, he would let that all be in the dark recesses of his mind, he was here to check her out. With the first glance of her, all his doubts vanished.

The years had been good to her physically for she was as he remembered, only better. She had grown maybe an inch or two and added fifteen pounds, which did not detract from her appearance at all. There was that same great smile and genuine warmth he always felt when he was around her. It was truly marvelous to see her again. He wanted desperately to hold her in his arms until everything in the past dissipated and all the pain and misery was gone. He knew his life had taken a turn for the better now that he had met with her again.

"Yvonne, you look terrific," he greeted her.

"O, thanks, I would recognize you too," she smiled back. They both stood there holding hands and looking at each other. She thought, *This would be a perfect scene for time to stand still.*

"Shall we go in and have a seat?" he asked. "We have a lot to catch up on." He held onto her hand as they entered the restaurant looking as a happy couple. Yvonne was so relieved that their meeting came off so well. She had wanted the hug, and now holding his hand brought warmth, and forgiveness, and gave her chills all at the same time.

They talked and smiled. They talked and laughed. They talked for hours. She realized how much she had missed this kind of relationship, the easy comfortable way each felt, and the way they could so easily converse with each other. Why had they taken the paths that they did? Why had she stopped writing him? Where was all this going to lead? All this excitement was all so weird, but she could hardly hide her enthusiasm or even keep up with her own thoughts.

The conversation went from her life to his life, then back again. She repeated the information she had conveyed to his mother that she had been married for about twelve years, had four children and was now divorced. Joe said he too had married, lived in Oklahoma, had two children and was now divorce. After two hours of non-stop chatter, Yvonne said, "I'm sorry to say, but I have to get home to the children."

"Oh no," replied Joe, "I guess I need to get going also, but can I see you again?"

"Yes, you surely may," she smiled.

"I will call you as soon as I return from this trip." Joe hugged her as they stood by her car and then he walked to his truck, turning to give her a smile. Yvonne continued to watch him as he pulled away. The thought in her mind kept saying, "Why? Why had her life progressed as it had with David instead of with Joe?"

She sat there for a minute recalling the evening from the first sight of Joe to now. She wondered just what she had missed in the past years since they had parted. It was more of a dream than reality being here tonight with Joe. What chance was there that they would meet again after twelve years of not knowing anything about each other? Being with this gorgeous person for a short time tonight, was as if the years had never passed between them. How could that be? Yvonne urged herself to put the car in gear to drive home. Of course, she was smiling with many good memories spinning in her mind. Where do we go from here?

Chapter XVI

Joe's enlistment into the Navy had not been his idea at all. After lengthy discussion with his parents, his father insisted that he enter some form of military service since he did not desire to go back to school. His father thought the service was the better way to go to promote Joe's growth. Joe hadn't told Yvonne the details about the decision only that his father had pushed it upon him. At the time, he just told her about signing up and how he would be leaving in two weeks. He really wasn't all that excited about it, but tried to impress her that it was a good thing. It had seemed reasonable to Yvonne, so she assumed that it was a good decision since her brothers had been in the services also, and it had worked for them.

Joe missed home and life as he knew it before the Navy. He tried to do all that he was required, but wasn't into excelling at anything. He made friends yet could only concentrate on Yvonne and always imagined as to what she might be doing back home. He loved receiving every letter from her. Even though she said she missed him, she always wrote how much fun she had at school. Joe just couldn't understand how she enjoyed school so much. Her letters caused him to feel good but also feeling left out of her life.

How could he survive away from her so long? He wrote to her as much as he could, but hardly knew what to write about except how much he missed her and loved her.

Getting time away from the service, to go home to see Yvonne were the happiest days he had. He realized he had to comply with the regulations and do his best at the exercises to earn some leave time. This he was willing to do. Each leave he attained, he eagerly made arrangements to get home to see her the fastest way he could manage. He loved to surprise her with his visits. Spending a day or two with her gave him the energy to carry on when he got back on base.

In his visits home, he always asked her to marry him; she answered, "No." It put a little crack in his heart each time. Why wouldn't she give in and just say yes? He really didn't have any ideas as to how they would live as husband and wife, or where, he just thought he wanted to be married to her. He thought of nothing else. When the guys in service with him went out for the weekend, he had a hard time going with them, because he just wanted to be with Yvonne.

He had wanted so much to have sex with Yvonne, but he didn't want to take advantage of her. Besides, with both of them being virgins, it was too difficult to initiate the process. They came close. It would have been easy since they loved each other so much, but he thought she would rather be married before they did it, and he wanted to keep her happy. Did she not understand how hard it was for him to withhold this important part of love? He would wait for her. He hoped and prayed that she would wait for him also.

He tried to think of ways to get her to commit to marriage. His best idea was to buy a ring to give to her, thinking it could possibility convince her. The men in his barracks agreed that was a great way to show her he was serious. He was very excited to make the purchase and surprise her, hoping that it would surely convince her to promise to become his wife. How disappointing when she once again said, "No." *Yvonne, you really cannot be serious! Oh God, why? Why can she not say yes?*

Joe was really on a downhill slide after Yvonne said she would not wear the ring or marry him. It was driving him crazy to be away from her and even worse that she rejected his proposal. He had trouble doing his work. He had trouble sleeping. He had trouble adjusting to time, the duties he had to perform, and waiting. What could he do? He would not give up. Her letters were coming farther apart and fewer in number. He had trouble writing to her without commenting about his hope for marriage and why wouldn't she marry him?

About the worst day of his life, which he will always remember, he received a letter no man ever wants to get. She wrote to him that she doesn't want to be his girl anymore! No! *No, Yvonne, don't ever say that!* Joe just could not believe what the letter contained. He left his cabin on the ship and went to the open deck. He stood there by the railing with the letter in his hand, tears rolling down his cheeks. The moon rose, the stars came out, he remained starring at the ocean, the moon, and the stars, with the memory of Yvonne's face in his mind. She was in his heart forever. He knew that she always would remain in his heart, but he just couldn't visualize her not being a part of him.

He read the letter again hoping that he had misread before. In his wallet was the picture of Yvonne and himself that his sister had taken the first time she came to his house. He took the picture out and starred at it. He could do nothing at this moment to change her mind, to retain her friendship, to have her reclaim the letter she had written. He was in the middle of the ocean on a ship without a single way to contact her. So he just stood there, staring, remembering, and crying silent tears of love.

Joe did write to Yvonne again, asking her to please change her mind. She answered his letter, but did not relent on her position. She told him there was not someone else in her life, but she just needed to feel free to live her life as best as she could. A couple more letters spaced out over a couple of months and then he let it go. Not so much in his heart, but with the letters and pleadings.

Why? He asked himself over and over again. He thought his time in the service was hard being away from Yvonne, but now it was even more painful knowing that she was not waiting for him, writing him, loving him. He did his chores as instructed but his actions were not with his whole heart. Every day was another lonely day on a big ship with a bunch of guys whom he did not dislike, but just did not want to be there.

Finally, Joe's time of service in the Navy ended! Hooray, now he could go home. He was very tired of living on a ship, seeing so much water every day. He was ready to live again on land close to family.

Shortly after his return home, visiting family, and adjusting to regular life, he set about trying to find out where Yvonne was and what she might be doing after time had passed. He heard that she was engaged to be married, but he didn't know how soon. He stopped in at the tavern down on the corner of the town where she lived. Visiting with the nice lady owner, she informed him of Yvonne's situation. She really didn't know if Yvonne was happy about the coming marriage, but she thought things were going pretty well.

Joe contemplated on what she had told him. He wanted desperately to see Yvonne, but was afraid to intrude on her life. He sat there for quite a while, debating what to do. Finally, he exited the building, got into his car, almost made a right hand turn to go see Yvonne, but ultimately made a left hand turn and drove away from the tavern, from the village, from Yvonne.

Joe tried to get something going with his life as far as a job, career, friends, and where to live. This was all very different now since Yvonne was no longer in the plans. He worked a couple of different jobs without really liking any of them. He decided to try driving a semi-truck, thinking he could do that without any problems. It worked. With this new position, he was earning money enough for a car and to live on. Not that he really needed a place to live when he was on the road most all the time. With time off, he would visit his mom, keeping their relationship alive. What would he do with his life now? He had a few dates with a couple different girls whom he had met around his old home town. Not one of them could dissolve the memory of Yvonne. For one thing, he did not want to forget about Yvonne, although he knew and everyone said that was what he needed to do. Try as he might, she was always on his mind.

Then one night, Joe met a girl, Mollie, who seemed like a nice person, not too much unlike Yvonne. They had a few dates, got along pretty well, beginning a new relationship for both of them. He did not want to be alone or lonely anymore, so it wasn't long until he asked Mollie to marry him. Mollie was happy with Joe's attention, so even though they hadn't known each other very long, she accepted his proposal. They rented a home, gathered some furniture together, and began their life as a married couple.

In less than a year, they welcomed a baby girl. Joe loved his little girl. She was beautiful, sweet, and perfect as far as he was concerned. He thought his marriage to Mollie was pretty good, except Yvonne was still in his heart and the picture of the two of them was still in his billfold. Joe and Mollie soon started having a few problems though, mainly because his paycheck just wasn't enough to cover all the expenses of their new family. Joe wasn't happy about that either. He talked to some other guys about a better job.

One fellow offered news of better paying truck driving jobs in Oklahoma. Joe checked out the information, proceeded with an application, and was hired. So he left his home state going to Oklahoma, beginning a new truck driving career traveling across the states. As soon as he could afford it, he went back home to get his wife and baby. They set up housekeeping in a new state, with a new job, and tried to settle in. Life wasn't too bad in Oklahoma. Joe's income was enough most of the time.

The problem of living in a state away from family and friends is that one can feel isolated and miss seeing family. Mollie knew no one and was shy about trying to meet new people. Joe preferred that she remain at home with their child. Mollie loved her little girl and poured lots of time and attention toward her, however, this devotion didn't keep the loneliness away. Joe got lonely too being out on the road a week at a time. They both tried to deal with their loneliness without much success.

Mollie became pregnant again which produced a son, whom they named Joey. This son also presented Joe much pride and happiness. He loved being a father of two beautiful children, sometimes splurging too much on the children, causing friction with Mollie. Worse than that, she felt trapped at home with the children, with no friends or relatives near to spend time with. She did her chores and grocery shopping in the small town with little connection with other people. Then this fellow began to speak to her. Each week he continued his pursuit to get to know her. It was nice to have conversation with an adult.

Mollie didn't know how to handle this situation, but she did like the attention. She didn't intend to hurt Joe, but she felt she had to make a change in her life. This new acquaintance in her life was kind to her and available, as Joe was not. Joe had no idea about this man until his little girl slipped a few words about Mommie's friend. Joe got terribly angry and greatly distressed. They argued. Mollie apologized to Joe, and he gradually calmed down.

The next time he was gone on a trip, Mollie packed clothing for herself and the children and left. When Joe came home to an empty house, he knew not where they were. After many phone calls trying to find them, he got word from a friend where his family might be. Joe made contact with Mollie. He begged her to come back home, but she refused. Joe became violently angry, threatening to harm this man. Police got him to leave unless he preferred to go to jail. Mollie proceeded with divorce papers. Joe did not desire this, nor did he ever expect something like this to happen. He was distressed, angry, and depressed for a long time. Work was the only thing that kept him going. He had a very difficult time contacting Mollie when he wanted to see the children. He continued driving truck, living for the next time when he could see his children again. This was his life for a while.

Working a lot, staying in motels, trying to see his children when he could, Joe was just about to throw in the towel. He didn't know what to do from day to day. Driving a truck presented him with plenty of time to think about his children, life, and future. Trying to keep himself out of depression, he confided with his mother on the phone almost every day. Finally, he took some time off to visit his mother. This was a good idea for them both. They could always have a discussion on any problem, even the most sensitive subject was easy for them. This visit turned out to be the best one which they had for a long time, for Joe appreciated all that his mother had to say.

But now he had to make some decisions as to what he might do with his present situation. Missing his children terribly, even with the judge's decree that he could see them, Mollie made it difficult for Joe. Finally, he made a very hard choice. He quit his job in Oklahoma and moved back home close to his parents and family. Contacting Mollie was very difficult as she changed phone numbers and moved frequently. He would never give up any kind of relationship with his children, but had to give Mollie distance for now.

Chapter XVII

Reuniting with Joe was indeed good for Yvonne, as she felt more alive, able to retract parts of her younger self. Their broken relationship mended quickly, by telephone conversations taking place almost daily. Each time they were together, conversation flowed with great smiles and quiet moments. There was never any condemnation on the part of either one about any event in the past. They both wanted their pasts to be gone and forgotten.

Joe conveyed to Yvonne parts of his life since they had parted. "Shortly after you married, I found a girl who I thought I could be happy with and we married. We hardly knew each other, but made the leap anyway. Our marriage progressed in some ways as yours." He continued on with some reluctance. "I began driving truck just after I was home from the service. I hauled many different products from cattle to vegetables, to gasoline all over the states for the past ten years or more. I did enjoy living in Oklahoma, once I grew accustomed to it. The atmosphere and people were likable, but we were totally on our own away from all family." He stopped talking while looking her in the eyes, then said, "Enough for now. Let's go for a walk."

After such conversations with Joe, Yvonne thought they had enough information about their past marriages, that each could assess the situation and move forward in a positive direction. Anyway, she decided that age thirty-one, Joe was a nice-looking young man, as much or better as before. His hair was a little longer now so that it had some curl to it and the additional mustache, only gave him a more distinguished look. He now wore cowboy boots, a custom gained from living in Oklahoma and she noticed the cuffs on his long-sleeved shirt were tucked under instead of over, to make it appear as a three quarter length sleeve. Yvonne had seen her father do this with his long sleeve shirts, so she was pleased with Joe's style having the same neat look.

What else was different about him now? She wasn't sure because in her eyes, he still looked handsome and being with him caused her to feel better. She waited for him to share anything else of his past, never asking or prodding. The most regret he had, which caused him the most suffering, was the fact that he did not have enough time with his two children. She understood that, but thought it profound at the amount of heartache he carried because of not being with them.

Joe was amazed at how great Yvonne looked. He was elated to see her after all the years, and realizing that she wanted to see him, gave him a warm confident feeling. He had never lost his admiration for her, nor the longing he felt for her through the years. Joe looked forward to each meeting with Yvonne, to learn all about her life during the time that they were apart, and he was anxious to meet her children, for he did love children. Yes, he liked children and it was hurting him not to be able to see his own children more often. He liked to please the kids with toys and fun things to do.

As he traveled on the road, Joe tried to imagine what life would be like with Yvonne once again. Certainly, time with her must be better because his heart had a sincere desire to be with her and to love her with all his body and soul. Their recently renewed acquaintance was filling his thoughts with new desire that he had lost since his own divorce. Even though his marriage had been a rocky mess for most of the years, he still thought he would like to be married and have a family. He realized that to be a true fact for him especially since meeting with Yvonne again.

On the weekend, when Joe had a couple days off, Yvonne invited him over to the house to meet the children and have dinner with them. When Joe arrived at the house, the children were a little apprehensive as to who he might be and why he was at their house. Yvonne explained to them, "This is my friend from a long time ago. His name is Joe, and he came to visit us and meet you." The children were certainly looking him over with questions on their faces. "Joe, this is Dolly, this big boy is Jesse, here is Sissy, and little guy is Jacob."

Joe smiling shook Dolly's hand, saying, "You look like my girl Tess," then shook hands with Jesse, and patted Sissy and Jacob on the head and commented, "Joey is a little bigger than you."

Dolly spoke, "Where is your girl?"

Joe replied, "She lives in Oklahoma with her mother, just as you live with your mother." He said, "I will bring Tess and Joey to meet you all soon. Would that be good?"

They all nodded yes, and scattered in different directions to resume play.

Joe slowly interceded in playing with them, quickly making friends with each one as the day progressed. His love for children showed in his actions and words. He told them about his children and about life in Oklahoma. Yvonne saw right away that she had no need to worry about Joe getting along with them. He watched cartoons and played a game, encouraging Yvonne to join in. She did and they had a very good day. Dinner was pleasant and soon the evening came to a close. Before Joe left, he asked the children, "May I come back again?"

Dolly and Jesse answered, "Yes, you can." Yvonne walked Joe out to his car. He hugged her. "Thank you for dinner," he whispered and kissed her with a smile, checking to see if the children were looking.

She smiled as she said, "Goodnight." Joe drove down the lane as she breathed a sigh of relief that the day had gone so well. Walking back into the house she smiled and called out, "Are you all in bed?"

"Yes, Momma," Sissy replied. She kissed each one and sat down to reflect on what had transpired today and in the past weeks since connecting with Joe. She felt quite relieved with all of it in contrast to the way she had been feeling the last couple of months.

The next time Joe came over, while the children were visiting their father, Yvonne and Joe made a trip to visit her parents to announce their reunion. Of course, her parents were greatly surprised to see Joe again after so many years. This newly recreated relationship caused concern for them, but they could see the smile on her face, giving them relief that this might be something good. Her parents had been quite worried about their daughter since David had left her, but were confident that she would be able to take charge of her life and raise her children somehow, although they knew not how she would accomplished such a feat.

So far, it appeared that she was making a good effort to do all that she could. They were uncertain how Joe might fit in after all the years apart, plus the addition of four children. They had seen how some marriages fell apart time and again as was the case with her father's siblings. They just wanted Yvonne and her children to be happy. They made no judgment or criticism as to the new relationship.

It was a nice afternoon with her parents. Her father and Joe were able to talk about driving truck with many of the experiences her father had. Upon leaving the house, they drove around town so Joe could once again visualize where their footprints had been left long ago. The little town had changed in many ways, but for the most part, it appeared the same to them after all this time. They went pass Joe's uncle's house, which was empty, pass the grocery store, and of course, the swimming hole, where they spent many a summer day. These were some of their favorite places which provided many happy memories. Driving along the country road, they were talking and laughing about their youthful days.

Joe smiled as he spoke, "Remember the day we spent swimming, and as we walked home, you felt so sick?"

Yvonne blushed as she replied, "Oh yes I do. I was really scared for a little while. A piece of bread never tasted so good!"

Joe commented, "You sure had me scared. I didn't know what to think or what we should do."

They approached a turn in the road where Joe should have turned left, but instead he went right. This was another country road which eventually came to a dead end where one of Yvonne's girlfriends had lived long ago. She looked at Joe with questions as he pulled over in the edge of the timber before the road made another turn. Joe stopped the car, and got out. It was a quiet wooded area which no one used much anymore. Yvonne was pretty sure that no one lived back here, and if anyone came by, they would see them coming.

The sun shone brightly on the autumn colored trees as she walked up beside him where he leaned on the car. Joe slid his arm around Yvonne, hugging her tightly. She looked him in the eyes as they kissed. She smiled at him as she wondered what he might have in his mind. The day had been very pleasant from the beginning, so this particular action only added to the pleasure. The sun glowed through the trees, while a few colorful leaves fell around them. He began to kiss her several times with the kisses becoming more passionate. Pulling her closer, he reached under her skirt, feeling the smoothness of her thigh. She felt the warmth of his body, the smell of his cologne, and the beat of his heart. His embrace lifted her off the ground to allow his entrance into her.

Yvonne's body was suddenly set ablaze with more stimulation than she had ever experienced. The excitement between them became hotter than the sun shining through the trees. The gentle physical movement brought forth the expressions of desire from both of them. What an amazing encounter after so many years of waiting! She had never imagined sex could be so exciting, warming, and thrilling. He held her tight as she wrapped her legs around him. They were together at last! This was what she had been missing all those years! This day now consummated their previous lives and the present as if there had never been a void. Their love from the very beginning so many years ago was brought to life, to blossom, grow, and live eternally.

Yvonne could only stare into his eyes, reflecting back to a previous magical night of walking in the snow, when her heart had been filled with loving peace back then. Now the excitement of today revived that peacefulness within her. Their hearts opened to each other in every way. They had much to look forward to. It all felt so right, so long in coming, so welcomed.

They stood there face to face allowing their bodies to calm, starring into each other's eyes. "I love you, Yvonne," Joe whispered. "Do you love me?"

"Yes, I do."

"I think I better sit down before my legs give way," he chuckled. They moved inside the vehicle, sat there for a while, basking in the sun, warmth, and love they were feeling, not ever wanting to lose what they had found today.

Upon arriving at Yvonne's house, he kissed her then said, "I should go."

She took his hand in hers as they walked into the house, retreating to the bedroom, holding each other, loving each other, snuggling all through the night.

Chapter XVIII

Joe always spoke of his children with love and pride, even though he saw them so infrequently. Of course, their mother had custody and always seemed to make it difficult for Joe to be in touch with them on a regular basis. Tears would fill his eyes when he spoke of them. Clearly anyone could see how much he loved and missed his children, as his heart was heavy with sadness. His visits with them were so sporadic and short, partly because his occupation of driving truck was not always a regular routine, and the children were in school, so this too kept visitation very minimal. Yvonne wondered how and when this situation could possibly be corrected.

Joe picked Yvonne up from work on Friday evening to dine out. She sat next to him as he drove through town. Out of the blue, Joe asked her, "Could you reach into the back to retrieve my jacket which has fallen on the floor?"

"Sure," she said as she turned toward the back, saw the jacket on the floor, and reached to pick it up. As she lifted the jacket, she saw yellow roses! What a surprise! "Whatever are these for?" she gasped with amazement.

"Because I love you, because I like being with you, because you are special to me," answered Joe.

Yvonne hugged him and kissed him the best she could without causing him a problem with driving. This was the greatest, best gift she had ever received from anyone in her life. Joe sure was pouring out his heart toward her and she was learning how to accept and give love back. Their evening together was again a time of joy, happiness, and love. She appreciated the dozen yellow roses very much, but also the tactic he used to present them was the best surprise. These times with Joe were bringing much joy to her life each day. She soaked in all his attention, attitude, and gratitude for her. She thought she did not deserve all this from him, but certainly was happy to receive it.

Even with all the good moments shared with Joe, Yvonne was still concerned with the thought of a second marriage. It was now less than six months since her divorce from David. The memories of struggle, sadness, and fear had not disappeared from her mind. She realized that maybe she had messed up big time by not marrying Joe in the first place, but she just didn't want to make another big mistake. She wanted more time to think about this new relationship, and also, since it involved her children, she wanted them to have time to adjust to the changes they were experiencing.

One day, Yvonne received an unexpected call from her ex-sister-in-law, Jean. "Yvonne, I'm sorry to carry bad news, but I thought you should be warned of David's plan. He has decided the relationship with your new friend is detrimental to the children and he is going to take action to try to remove them from your care." Evidently, David did not like seeing Yvonne with another man.

Dumbfounded, Yvonne mumbled, "What, why does he care? He left us." This plan of his shocked her to the point of anger. She didn't want to lose her position as full time parent. "Why does he think he can live his life as he pleases, but I cannot?" Yvonne stammered.

Jean answered, "I know, but he has assumed that Joe has moved in with you, which has not met with his disapproval."

"First of all, Joe has not moved into my house, and second, I can have a friend without David's approval," she continued as her anger mounted.

"Well, I just wanted to warn you. My thought was that if you were to marry soon, David would not have a solid reason to go forth with this plan, and therefore put an end to his scheme to mess with your life, and the lives of the children. Do what you think is best, I just was concerned about what he had in mind. I thought I should warn you, sorry."

"I see. Thanks, Jean, for calling. I appreciate your caring." She hung up the phone, thinking she might explode. *How could he be so brazen? He goes off with a married woman, and expects me to stay single? He cannot control my life, but I have to be aware of how I live to ensure the safety and responsibility of my children. He left us! He should leave me alone.*

Later that day, speaking to Joe, she explained the situation. Joe was sorry to see Yvonne upset. "What do you want to do?" he asked.

"I don't know, I am afraid he might actually try to do what he says. I don't want any trouble. I don't want to lose custody of my children. He will not care for them as I do," she rambled on.

Joe lifted her chin gently, looking into her tear-filled eyes, and said, "We could get married."

She tried to smile, "I know, but I didn't want to rush."

"It's alright with me, Yvonne. You know I love you." Joe kissed her on the cheek.

"Thank you. Let's talk about it some more when I can think better."

Because of this situation and for this reason, Yvonne's and Joe's marriage plans became more prominent. If marriage could avert a ridiculous situation and keep David from pursuing the process of removing the children from her care, she would definitely consider getting married.

After several days of discussing the situation with Joe, Yvonne called the minister from the church to discuss the matter with him. She respected him and would value his opinion. After work, she went to his home to explain her delicate situation. He listened as she explained about her new relationship with Joe, how they knew each other from the past, and what David threatened to pursue at this time. He asked a few questions, and reported of incidents in his personal life that related. He processed the information for a bit, and said, "I think it would certainly be suitable for you and Joe to marry. In fact, we could do it today or tomorrow if you prefer not to wait."

Wow! This idea was totally unexpected coming from Reverend Henry. Yvonne called Joe to convey the news to him. Joe was pleased with this information. Since their last conversation to proceed with marriage plans in the near future, Joe had applied for marriage license. He went immediately to the courthouse to pick them up.

It was almost no time at all that Joe arrived at the minister's house, where the three of them had a serious consultation. This conversation helped counter most of Yvonne's fears as to what David would be able to do as far as the children were concerned. Yvonne didn't know if she was ready for this marriage thing again, but that was exactly what they did.

Joe and Yvonne became husband and wife finally after all the years of being apart since their first meeting in 1961. Right there in the preacher's house, they said their vows. It was exciting. It was scary. It was sweet to be married to Joe. The minister, his wife, Joe and Yvonne, wearing just what they had on, was all it took. They were married! Perhaps everyone would be happy, and Joe and Yvonne could fulfill their promise to each other for many years to come.

It was thrilling to be in love, to be married to someone you are happy to be near. This new life for them filled with much happiness and love. They were wrapped in each other's arms every night they were together. Yvonne smiled every day, with only a small amount of trepidation of what David might come up with next. He still made a feeble attempt to remove the children from her care, but the plan failed before going to court, as Yvonne had a lot of support from family and friends as her defense.

It was only a few more days until the Thanksgiving holiday. Joe made final arrangements to pick up Tess and Joey for the holiday. "Yvonne, would you go with me to pick up my kids?" he asked with much enthusiasm. He was as excited as a youngster headed out to trick or treat. "It would give me much happiness if you would." She accepted, so the two of them figured out a plan to fetch his children.

This was Yvonne's first time to visit Oklahoma, but also the first time meeting Joe's children. Would she like them? She thought that she definitely would connect with Joe's two children as Joe had with hers. She was not too worried about their meeting, only a little anxious. The fall day began fairly warm for November, as they began their journey west. Joe pointed out places of interest on the route as Yvonne enjoyed the scenery. Their travel was not boring at all, as they continuously conversed about their children, about parents and siblings, and of their younger days when they had fallen in love the first time.

When there happened to be a moment of silence, Yvonne would sometimes sing along with the radio. That was something she had not done much of in years past being with David, since he didn't approve of her music style or her singing. Joe smiled at her, giving her the courage to continue. Joe's choice of country music, which he acquired while living in Oklahoma, brought back memories to Yvonne of traveling with her father. His favorite music was country also.

Joe knew all the country western singers and all their songs. His life in Oklahoma for several years had transformed him from a rural kid into a real western guy.

Anyway, he liked being thought of as such. Yvonne was cool with that image. She had to listen to some songs memorizing the words as fast as possible to catch up with Joe's library of country music. She also remembered that her family had always liked music, so why had she let David keep her from enjoying any of it? Her spirit rose higher as Joe encouraged her to continue with the music as the miles clicked by.

It was early evening as they arrived in the town of their destination. Joe parked the car in front of a small building that appeared to be a bar. He took her hand as they walked through the door, where it was very quiet since hardly any other customers were present. He selected a table for them, ordered a couple of drinks, and made several choices on the jukebox, filling the quiet room with music. Their conversation continued. Joe had much to tell Yvonne about his life in Oklahoma. They felt relaxed in this quiet place, talking and listening to a good selection of country music for about an hour, unaware of anyone else in the world, as they enjoyed each other's company.

Grateful for a wonderful day, and anticipation of seeing his children tomorrow, kept Joe's spirits high. Many of the great country singers were filling the room with their love songs. A very familiar one started to play which the words matched up with their relationship. Joe got up from his chair, took Yvonne's hand, and led her out onto the floor in front of the juke box. He pulled her close as they began to move slowly around the floor. She felt his warmth as she leaned against his body as she was held in the arms of her loving man. There was no one else in the world except the two of them.

Their bodies moved together as one and their hearts melted into the biggest circle of love that anyone could imagine. Yvonne could not have enjoyed a dance with anyone any more than she did at that moment. She wished that more days of her life would have been like this one, and prayerfully hoped there would be more in the future. The music ended, they walked out the door hand in hand with love in their hearts, stars in their eyes, and happiness beyond expression.

Rising the next morning after a loving night together, quickly became a big deal. Both were nervous and excited as they arrived at the home where his daughter and son were living with their mother. Joe's face became animated as he smiled happily advancing toward the children who came rushing out to greet their father. Yvonne could see the love he held for his children pouring out of him like rays of sunshine. She could not have selected two children to be more like her own.

His daughter was tall, thin, with long dark hair very much like Dolly's. His son was smaller built, shy, and cute as a button. He looked just like Joe and of course, was named after him. Joe introduced them to Yvonne, but as pleasant as they were to her, they were most happy to see their father. She didn't mind. They missed him and were totally glad to be with him again. Once they packed their luggage in the car, they were off for Illinois. It was easy to see how much Tess adored her father, and little Joey wanted to be with him too.

Tess and Joe talked for most of the trip. Yvonne listened to their conversation, learning about his children by words spoken, and witnessing their adoration. It was quite a while before they settled a bit. This trip to Oklahoma appeared to be a worthwhile venture. Yvonne could easily see the happiness and love in Joe's eyes and heart for his children. She was happy for him to have this time with Tess and Joey.

Joe was feeling very happy as he, Tess, and Joey visited a couple days with their grandparents, making it a wonderful time for Grandma and Grandpa. It was happiness for them too, getting reacquainted since the children were growing so fast. After visiting with Joe's parents for a few days, he brought the children to Yvonne's house to meet her children. Joe proudly introduced Tess and Joey to Dolly, Jesse, Sissy and Jacob.

It took very little encouragement for all of them to skip formalities, they were off and playing like children often do. The six of them took to liking one another as if they had known each other for quite a while. The girls bonded quickly and the boys joined ranks against the girls. What a fun time they had. Yvonne celebrated the addition to her family with pride. Whenever Joe wanted the children to do something, he would say, "Andale, andale." The girls giggled as they all looked at him.

Dolly asked, "What does andale mean?"

Tess answered, "It means go ahead in Spanish, or hurry." So they did go in a hurry, laughing all the way.

The time spent with Joe and his children, passed quickly, but made for a very good holiday. Thanksgiving with Joe's family was pleasantly appreciated by Yvonne, and Joe loved her even more for making this time so great.

Each day was filled with fun activities playing games, eating ice cream, and laughing a lot. Joe introduced tacos and burritos to all which was a new taste for her family. Of course, everyone loved pizza!

The days seemed much too short, as it was time for Joe to make the trip back to Oklahoma, returning his children to their mother. He had no desire to do that. His heart felt very heavy as he packed the children's bags into the car to begin their journey. Yvonne could again see the love he held in his heart for them, and how difficult this was for him to take them home to Oklahoma. Yvonne could not make this return trip with Joe because of work and caring for her own children. So even though everyone enjoyed a wonderful holiday together, Joe was still saddened that it had to end.

Yvonne had experienced a totally different family situation than any before. Divorce, single parenting, and caring for little ones added to this life a new chapter. One she was not sure how to process, but so far each day progressed with positive effects.

Preparing for Christmas this year was a much easier and fun chore. Joe loved the idea of Christmas, buying gifts, decorating, helping Yvonne with all that he could. She was not accustomed to much sharing in preparations. Her new family enjoyed a good Christmas even though many changes and adjustments had evolved, which some were good and others more difficult. Joe surprised her with a new Bible, which she thought was very thoughtful. It was actually her first very own, for she had always been using one belonging to her older brother. Joe couldn't have been any happier unless his own children could be with him all the time, but he still gave every effort to please others. Yvonne was satisfied that maybe this is how her life would be from now on.

Chapter XIX

By stipulation of the divorce decree, now that Yvonne had remarried, she was required to move out of the house, or begin to pay rent. Yvonne and Joe discussed the possibilities of staying where they were, moving closer to family, or go somewhere else. They both agreed that staying where they were was not suitable for anyone. The house was owned by David, it was four miles from the school, twelve miles from Yvonne's work, and totally out of the path for Joe's commute. It was a house on farmland which was the place David and Yvonne had chosen just two years before. It just did not benefit Yvonne in her new situation. It was definitely too close for David to watch over her every move. They must move.

Joe came up with a very big idea! Yvonne could not even fathom what he was suggesting! It was just too much of a change for her. He suggested the family move to California, where he was sure he could operate an over the road truck service and provide a living for them. Yvonne was terrified of moving so far away from her parents, family, and taking the children so far from their father.

They discussed his plan every day and every night, until they could at least see the possibility of it working. Joe was confident that this would be a good solution to a new place to live, and also his occupation could best thrive. She discussed their plan with her brother, Daryl, who lived in California, and he gladly agreed to help get them situated once they made the move. Arrangements for the move began immediately. A rental truck was located and loaded with everything that could possibly be squeezed in. They said good bye to all family and on the second day of a new year began their journey to a new adventure.

This was going to be a whole new life for the six of them. Dolly, Sissy, Jesse, and little Jacob were excited with the idea, which, Joe painted a wonderful picture that sounded undeniably fantastic. It would definitely be a challenge to change Yvonne's way of life as she knew it. She had never imagined living so far from Illinois. Joe drove the truck while Yvonne followed in the car.

The children switched riding in the truck and then the car. It was quite a goal for her to drive the long distance, but all went well. The children were awed by the mountains, the desert, and change in the weather. Yvonne had made a visit to her brothers' once before, but never drove, and had slept part of that journey. This time there was no sleeping while traveling, except they did stop late at night and took a long nap in the car.

Arriving in California at her brother's house, where they would stay until they could find living quarters of their own. This arrangement made it easier to transition. Daryl certainly was great support for her in this move. He became her safety net to the plan. He said their father always took care of family, so he would do the same. With Daryl's help, Joe found a semi-truck to purchase, arranged the first run, and was gone on the first delivery. Yvonne and the children stayed with her brother while she looked for a house.

It took a about six weeks, but Joe was the one who found a lovely place with a pool. Wow! The kids could hardly believe it, a swimming pool in the backyard. Yvonne could not believe they would live in such a nice house either. They moved their belongings into the house, as Joe teased, "Andale, andale." The children laughed and hurried as each carried something into the new house.

Everyone quickly settled into this new home, climate, and routine. Yvonne registered the children in school and busied herself with setting up housekeeping in her new California home. She was lonely while Joe was gone and never ventured far from their house. Shopping was done when Joe arrived back from a trip. She was always thrilled to have him home on each return. Their renewed love brought to their family a great joy. Joe only wished that his children could also be a part of this happy family.

It was usually warm in California, compared to Illinois, especially since summer had arrived. The months sailed by with Joe being gone most of the time, and now the end of the school year was here. Yvonne began supervising the children in the pool every day, which was an activity they had not been privilege to before. Marriage and living in California was progressing quite well.

Since moving the children so far from David, he requested the children visit with him to extend through the whole month of July. It was very difficult for Yvonne to imagine that long of a period without them. Never had she been away from them for so long. David met them at the airport, presenting the children with their very first flight on a commercial airline jet. As Yvonne watched them board the plane, she felt totally empty.

One time she had taken a trip without the children, and was homesick for them after just the second day. It was hard to be optimistic or happy. Joe suggested that she go on the truck with him for the month while the children were visiting their father. The thought of being at home alone did not appeal to her, so she packed a bag and went with him. It would be an adventure to travel in the truck with Joe, and see some country that she had never seen before.

On her first run with Joe, they travelled north through Washington on toward Oregon. Washington was awesome with so many tall trees. The delivery destination of goods, ended only four miles from Canada. Yvonne never dreamed she would see Canada, yet here she was so close. After reloading the trailer with new cargo, they continued across the northern states eastward to New York. That was a lot of miles of new country for her. Yvonne enjoyed the view, a time of change, and time with Joe. The boxes of apples were unloaded in Buffalo, and they proceeded south to New Orleans, which became a different type of landscape.

New York had been busy with people, buildings, and traffic, while New Orleans was very humid with rain showers. Much of the highways were built up over the swamp area like continual bridges. She was seeing a lot of interesting terrain. The next load which Joe picked up in New Orleans took them back through Illinois and on west to California, without time to visit family. This way of travelling presented many educational and fascinating sites, but her body was feeling strained from the lack of exercise.

As the days passed, she missed the children, but tried to keep her mind occupied. Days turned into weeks. Once again, they were back in California. They did not take time to stop at the house. Joe wanted to make as many runs in this month with Yvonne along as they possibly could. He had the trailer loaded once again, and drove toward Montana and North and South Dakota. It was amazing the amount of miles they were covering in the few weeks on the road.

Yvonne thought how great it was to be able to see so much country, which she probably wouldn't have visited otherwise, but she missed her children. She enjoyed being with Joe, learning how he set up his loads, seeing how efficiently he managed his time driving, and making each delivery to its destination. She gathered a very good picture of what Joe did on a daily basis. They talked the miles away and slept the nights together in the sleeper of the cab, which was definitely strange for her.

The lack of exercise weakened her physically and mentally. She started wishing to be home with her children, trying not to let Joe know how she was feeling. Joe realized how being homesick could affect a person and did all he could to keep her happy. She was not disappointed with the travel, but she was just getting truly homesick. Finally, the end of the month arrived as they ended their month-long journey in California. What an adventure it had been. She didn't want to seem ungrateful, but that much traveling had almost done her in!

It was a wonderful reunion picking up the children at the airport. They hugged their momma tight. Tears of joy filled Yvonne's eyes as she thought about how Joe, too, missed his children. From this past month, she understood a little more how it was for him to not have his children with him. Returning to their house, everyone took turns telling their story about the happenings of the last month. All in all, the conception of the conversation was about how they missed living in Illinois.

Yvonne and Joe missed their old home state also. Joe's children were still in Oklahoma, so it was hard for him to visit with them. Joe and Yvonne had further discussion about whether they would stay in California or return to Illinois. They really liked their new home with a beautiful pool, yet living here just did not seem natural for them. They soon made another big decision to return to Illinois, where they all wished to be. The move to California had not been a failure. It was a great adventure for the children, Yvonne, and Joe.

Joe was a bit disappointed to give up on his plan of working on his own, but realized it was not all about him. All plans were set in motion without further hesitation, the furniture was packed once again in a rental truck, and they made their way back to Illinois, where it felt like home.

Chapter XX

Returning to Illinois was difficult, as it seemed like they were starting over—from where?—starting from their first meeting, marriage, move from Illinois, or from California. First, they had to have a place to live. Somehow, Joe immediately found a house for rent in Graylawn. He amazed Yvonne with this ability to find what was needed. They quickly unloaded the truck, but did not unpack most boxes. Joe was very distressed from the packing, driving, unloading, and settling all the matters that needed attended.

Besides, he missed his children, so he decided to make a trip to Oklahoma. Yvonne was upset that he would leave her with basically a mess, so many unknown matters to settle, and many decisions to be made. He was dumping everything on her shoulders. It was understood that this house was a temporary rental, and they would have to move again soon.

Joe did not have another job lined up yet since returning. She worried how they would pay rent and even buy groceries. Joe wouldn't say how long he might be gone, which she realized that he didn't have any answers, just that he needed to see his children.

Yvonne kept very busy setting up the house enough so she could manage for a short while. She found a part time job, registered the kids for school, found a babysitter for little Jacob, and even managed to find another house to rent. Each day of not hearing from Joe caused her to worry and stress. Finally, she decided to call Mrs. Small, asking, "Have you talked to Joe? Do you know where he is or when he will return?"

"Yvonne, you know he went to see Tess and Joey. I have no idea when he might come back."

"I understand, I was just hoping you might have some answers for me. Sorry for being so brash. Please tell him I miss him, love him, and want him very much to hurry back."

"I will if I talk to him. Sorry too that he hasn't called you. Try to be positive."

"Thank you, I will. Thanks for your help."

Two days later, he returned feeling much better after the visit with his children. Yvonne accepted his explanations, trying to understand his pain and love for his children. They picked up where they had left off.

Joe looked for and found a job, not just a job, but a very good position. He found something better than ever before. This time he would be hauling new cars. This is great! He had acquired a good paying job with good insurance and benefits. Joe began his new job with much anticipation and excitement. Yvonne worked part time at the Catalog Store. It was all progress, making the best of each situation. Fall turned into winter as the days passed. Joe jumped off the car trailer one time and broke his ankle. Nuts! Insurance at work would cover it, so they just had to wait out his healing.

Christmas came a second time for them. Joe came up with a good idea for the boys' gift. He made a lay out on plywood for a race track, with trees, houses, railroad track, bridges, and roads. It was something he could work on while his ankle healed. Having completed this project, Joe and Yvonne had a fun time test driving the little cars around the track on Christmas Eve. This was a gift all the children enjoyed and played with. This was another good holiday with her family.

No one wanted to remain living in town in a rental house. Search for a house and property to buy was an ongoing task. A place was found which seemed to comply with their wishes. It was a three bedroom house with five acres in the country south of town. After inspecting the property and house, plans were put in motion to purchase this residence. Luck was with them. Everything worked out to their advantage, and they were able to buy the house. No family could have been happier or more excited.

Joe and Yvonne's marriage finally settled a bit. They had found a house they liked, both of them had jobs, her children were doing well in school, and they were happy and very much in love. This was pretty much what Yvonne had always dreamed of; family, home, and happiness. The goodness of the Lord was showering down upon them. One problem lingered for Joe of how much he missed his children. His heart yearned for them continually.

Joe was into a routine of making trips cross country delivering cars. Yvonne missed him a lot, but was able to work, care for the children, and do the necessary chores around the house. When Joe was home, they had good times, family time with her kids when they were home, and special time with each other when the children visited their father. The love they shared for each other grew each day as their time together could be pleasant, exciting, and loving. The biggest struggle Joe lived with was not having more contact with his two children. They could not find a good solution for this situation soon enough.

Epilogue

The next few days after the funeral remained busy, regardless of Yvonne's lack of energy to do anything. Joe's mother made arrangements to collect a few items of Joe's. It was hard to let go of anything that had been a part of Joe, but Yvonne didn't know what else she would do with his belongings. They talked, but casual conversation was all they could accomplish.

"Yvonne, the insurance policy is in Joe's children's names," Mrs. Small stated. "So the funeral will be paid out of that, because we know you can't afford to pay it."

Yvonne burst into tears hearing those words spoken. "Oh, thank you for doing that. Thank you so much."

"It's the least we can do. The rest of the money will be put into a fund for the children when they are older," she continued as she held Yvonne's hand.

"That is good," answered Yvonne. "I really appreciate all the help you have given me." That was the last time Yvonne saw Mrs. Small. They didn't say goodbye, but that was the ending.

This information about Joe's insurance was good and bad news to Yvonne. She had been waiting to hear from the insurance company herself. It came as a bit of a shock, yet somewhat a relief, even though she had thought the insurance would be in her name. She was expecting to receive the benefits to pay funeral expenses and to get her life on track again. She felt comforted, though, hearing this news from Mrs. Small, knowing that Joe's children would have something from their father when they needed finances for furthering their education or beginning their adult life.

She thanked God that the Smalls volunteered to pay the funeral expense, for she could not see any possible way she could financially afford it. She felt totally grateful, yet surprised that Joe had done that without even mentioning it to her. Anyway, that was the way it was, so she could live with that.

Yvonne also received a letter in the mail from the car insurance which stated that the truck Joe was driving at the time of the accident was fully insured and that she would be getting a new car in place of the truck. Tears rolled down her cheeks as she read the letter. It was amazing how things were being taken care of automatically without provocation or searching.

Social Security Administration notified her that she would receive a monthly amount for herself and for each of her children to provide for food, clothing, and shelter. All of these blessings came to Yvonne in response to and because of Joe's death. How much more could he have done for her? Of course, she would rather have him to be with her, but to receive these benefits from his passing were very much a blessing and seemed like such a loving gesture from Joe. It was with bittersweet joy that she managed to continue on without him.

Yvonne decided to continue working part-time. She needed to occupy every minute of her time now that Joe would no longer be around. With every blessing, she received, she felt that each one came from him. He had indirectly enabled her to continue living in the home which they had purchased, have a new vehicle to drive, and to feed her family. All these blessings flowed directly from his life. All this greatly relieved her worries of survival. None of it put her in the 'rich' category, but all things combined definitely kept her from having to depend on food stamps. There was such an irony about everything connected to her life. Before Joe came back into her life, she was struggling. Even after their marriage, they continued to struggle with jobs, a house, and vehicle. Now, it seemed that everything was somehow being taken care of for her.

Yvonne still did not understand how or why Joe had to leave her in this permanent fashion. The accident report stated that he had been drinking, and for some unknown reason had ran off the road crashing into a pile of hard dirt. Upon impact with the dirt, Joe fell over striking the back of his head on the glove box knob, causing him to bleed to death. It was over.

Yvonne knew that Joe had been in constant misery over not being able to see his children more. She knew he loved them more than anything. She knew Joe loved her. Why would he want to leave at this time? Perhaps he didn't plan to leave, but his story had come to an end. It must have been God's plan to take him home. She had to hold onto that thought so she could continue her life, and continue with raising her children.

She just didn't understand why Joe had to go. They had had so little time together. It was less than a year the first time that they were together as teenagers, and now it had been only two years that they had been married. Why so little time? Their love was as big as the universe and their time together so short. Yvonne could not rationalize what this relationship had been developed for, and then so rudely interrupted.

The past two years with Joe had not been the happiest for her, Joe, or the children. There were many decisions made, moves from Illinois and back, and trying to settle in a home. Yes, Joe and Yvonne were in love and happy to be married, but Joe constantly missed his daughter and son. Living with Yvonne's children only caused Joe to miss his children more. They both had regrets as far as the past, but accepted it as water under the bridge. It was hard to comply with the demands of the present day when you really wanted everything to be like it was a long time ago. Yvonne began to reminisce again and again…

Every time they had traveled together, Joe would drive and Yvonne would sit next to him and sing along with the radio. She was happy to be with Joe. He adored her, loved to see her happy. Singing was her way of expressing her happiness. One time singing a country song, Yvonne looked at Joe smiling for the words were similar to their lives. Joe understood what she was referring to as he smiled at her and nodded his head in agreement.

Whenever the children were visiting their father, Yvonne and Joe would always have mini honeymoons. Where ever they went or whatever activity they participated in, was like a honeymoon adventure to them. Sometimes he would surprise her with a special gift. One time he got her a locket with their wedding date inscribed on it. She never had anyone do this for her before. He got her a watch, perfume, a dress, a pair of shoes, a bathing suit, to name a few, but each item was special and treasured by Yvonne. He was her special country boy from the city, whom she loved with all her heart.

Each morning, Yvonne awoke with the remembrance of the dream of Jesus knocking on the door. It was kind of a calming reassurance that God was in control, reminding her that Joe loved her, even though Joe was not here anymore. She almost wanted to cry upon awakening, but after so many days of tears, one feels drained, empty, lost. She tried to keep her thoughts on her children each day, planning life as best she could for them, making it one step at a time.

She dressed, fixed breakfast, washed dishes, and then, and then…Oh, it was hard. Monday mornings were the hardest when the kids left for school. And then Friday nights were horrible when the children went to their father's and she was left alone, all alone. The tears would start and continue for hours. What could she do without Joe?

It had all started out so simply many years ago when she turned seventeen. They were innocent teens looking for the most important powerful part of their life to begin. Did they know what they had? *No*, she thought. *No, they certainly did not know*. Day after day she would go over in her mind trying to remember every detail, every incident, words spoken since the day they had met. How was it that after being apart for years, they got back together and then only eighteen months later, Joe was gone forever.

She knew no one could explain any of it. There would be no more love shared, no surprises, no more happy days shared between them. She talked to God, cried out her fears and loneliness to Him and then thanked Him for all that she had now and had shared with Joe.

Many days, she went over the last day of Joe's life in detail as much as she could remember. They had breakfast together, shared a tight hug and last kiss, she watched him back out of the drive. These little moments were what she had. After she received the news of the accident, all she had were questions in her mind. Why had Joe not called? Why did he stay out so late? Why didn't he make a haul on the truck? How had the accident happened?

Joe had gotten up early that morning, excited and ready to go back to work since his ankle had healed. Their new house was becoming their home. He enjoyed breakfast with Yvonne, as always. Joe carried some papers out to the truck and returning, saw Yvonne standing on the back door step. How he loved her! They kissed a sweet farewell, and he looked at her standing there as he backed out of the drive. He gave one last look at her thinking again how much he loved her. He arrived at the company doctor's office to get checked out and hopefully released to return to work. He anxiously waited some time for the doctor.

Finally, the doctor signed the release papers for him to work again, went to the main office with the release papers, handing them to the boss. He looked over the papers, checked with the delivery schedule, and got back with Joe. "Good news, Joe, you can return to work tomorrow."

Hurray! Joe was happy for that news, but had planned to leave on a trip that same day. "Sir," he said, "is there any way I could go out today?"

"No, you will have to wait until tomorrow."

Joe was disappointed as he walked out. He talked to a few other employees on the way. What was he going to do with the rest of the day? He knew Yvonne was working and the house would be empty. He didn't call Yvonne because she wasn't home. He contemplated his options. He could visit his mother, if she was home, return home and be alone, but none of these ideas attracted him. He took his time driving wherever he was headed.

He drove past his family's old home where he and Yvonne had spent some time. He drove to the village where he met Yvonne. This was where he met the girl of his dreams, and where he left her so many years ago. All great memories came to him. He stopped to have lunch and a beer at the local bar. It was pleasant talking to the people who were still running the place. After another beer, he headed on toward his home destination. On the way, he saw Wayne's truck parked at a bar he had frequented. He had time so he stopped in. They greeted each other and had a drink.

"Where have you been?" asked Wayne.

"Well I had a broken ankle which is now healed, and today, I just got released to go back to work tomorrow," Joe replied. They drank conversing about how he had broken his ankle. Joe continued, "It was my birthday too."

"Great," Wayne said, "have one on me." So they did. Meanwhile, another friend came in. They had a drink together. Shortly, Johnnie showed up after work so they had a drink. Time was flying without Joe even noticing. He should call Yvonne, but decided he would leave soon. Somehow he did not leave, but had another drink. Then someone else bought him a birthday drink. Joe thought he needed to go. It was getting late, he had drank too much already. He finally made his way out to the truck, thinking, *I should have left long ago. I should have called Yvonne. I'll just go home and surprise her. Man, I drank too much!*

Joe managed to get headed in the right direction. He thought, *What did I do? I should be home in bed with my love. Why didn't I call her? I am sorry, Yvonne. I am on my way, sweetheart. I will be there soon. I love you. I miss my kids. I'm sorry, Yvonne. Please forgive me. I'm coming, I'm coming.*

In his mind, he saw his children's faces as tears ran down his cheeks. He saw Yvonne waving at him to come to her. *Oh, Yvonne, I love you so much. I'm sorry I didn't come home sooner. I'm sorry I didn't call you, honey. I'm coming home, Yvonne. I love you. I'm coming. I'm coming.*